ALASTAIR M

STRIP OF LIGHT

AND OTHER SHORT STORIES

LOKI PRESS

Front cover illustration: *an Italian town with Christmas Lights.*

Published by

LOKI PRESS 2005

3 KING ST, KIRKWALL, ORKNEY, KW15 1JF

ISBN NO 0-9549751-1-1

Printed by
Graham and Sons
51 Gortin Road
Omagh
BT79 7HZ

Alastair Macleod is interested in everything but particularly in ordinary people and the issues they face in the modern world. In Strip of Light he explores how with hope, humour, the help of others and sometimes the mysterious guidance of nature, they manage to face those issues.

He likes willow pattern china and collects space memorabilia. He lives with his family in a remote but attractive part of Britain.

The Orkney Weather

CONTENTS

THE FALCON

Marco Falcone stood up from his desk and looked out over the Florence rooftops. You were supposed to take breaks from the screen – something about eyestrain.

On the block opposite, high up near the roof, kestrels had been nesting and he watched as one of the birds flew back to the nest and gently alighted. Part of him wanted to fly free like that.

He'd brought his binoculars in to work soon after he first noticed the pair. He was studying them when Andrea from Claims came in. "Bird watching again Marco?" she said rather suggestively. He swung round "At least the feathered kind don't wind you up in knots."

"Who's ever done that to you?" she queried in a bantering tone. She would like to know more about his love life, they all would. He was the new section head of Claims Control, a department directed to pay out as little as possible on behalf of the Avaro insurance company. The poor punters, if only they knew when they signed up that a whole department was geared up to deny their claim.

"I've one for you to look at" she said handing him a file. – "A bit up your street, I think" she smiled mysteriously.

Marco sat back resignedly at his desk. Difficult claims, in other words, ones difficult to refuse, came to him. A flood probably, or auto theft. He opened the file and began to read.

Pupella Spaccatini was claiming against her insurance for a new window in a listed building no less. What was interesting was that she claimed a pigeon, escaping from a bird of prey, had slammed into the window head on, "shattering it" she wrote, "like a windscreen."

The claim had already been part processed by his department. Comments on stickies, such as "a likely story" from Carlo, and "she's giving us the bird" by Andrea, were stuck to the fly leaf of the file.

Marco decided this merited a visit. A visit was not usually done. They were a paper crunching organisation and penny pinching too. He dreamed up some legal complications about expensive court cases that would worry his superior and hey presto he had approval to go up to Garfagnana in the Apuan alps to visit the claimant.

The staff were envious. There were comments of course. Donatella, the one with the heavy make up, was especially cynical. "Anything with wings gets you going Marco – a girl would have to be an Angel to come up to your standards." Marco smiled. What they didn't know was that just before he had joined Avaro his last relationship had ended disastrously.

Maria Beluzzi, his girlfriend of three years, had decided they were not compatible. She said it was his obsessive interest in birds. The truth was he wasn't that obsessive – he was nowhere near a twitcher, just mildly keen. Maria couldn't stand the competition. She was very emotionally demanding – wanted him either in each night or out with her. She went crazy when he went off by the banks of the Arno or to one of the parks in the city.

She once said, "You don't really care about me." He said, "Look," he countered "come with me, lets share this together," but she hated it. Too cold, too wet, too quiet. There was always something. He had loved her and he thought she had loved him, but one day he came home to the flat and she was gone. He joined Avaro the day after. Going back to the flat now was so depressing.

The next morning he was soon well up the autostrada, heading for Garfagnana. The claimant's home was just beyond it in San Lucche.

He found himself in winding back roads frequently stopping to check the map.

San Lucche was a small, tightly clustered hilltop village, surrounded by terraced vineyards descending to chestnut woods. The lady who answered the door was elderly. He had been half hoping that Pupella Spaccatini would be an artist in her late twenties or an earth mother.

As he went over the details with her she said the bird pursuing the pigeon had been a bird of prey, *a falco*, and, she was sure it had red tassels tied to its legs.

"Ah" he thought "a falconry bird".

"Was there a Falconry centre nearby?" he asked. "Yes" said Pupella "it opened last year – it's on the Cristaldi estate. I don't like it when they scare birds" she continued. Marco had noticed Pupella's bird table and feeders outside when he had inspected the window. Only the outer pane had shattered so there was no inside weather damage. After taking copious notes and reassuring Pupella that he had every reason to expect the claim to go through, he drove out of the village following Pupella's directions. The Falconry centre was located in a stable block next to the villa Cristaldi.

He could see the roosting cages off to the side. He strolled round and began peering at the birds – a Steppe Eagle, a Goshawk, then a Harris Hawk. Magnificent birds. "Can I help you?" said a female voice. A girl in a sleeveless olive green jacket, tan trousers and dark leather boots was addressing him. "Ehm, I'm from Avaro insurance." "Oh," She said "come into the office, it's a little warmer."

"You seem very interested " she continued, "My favourite is the Harris Hawk. She's very beautiful and works so well on a lure. We've only had her six months and she's the best at our field exhibitions."

"I see you have a Goshawk." Said Marco "Yes, he came to us via another Falconry that was closing down. He's full of character and works well." Marco noticed her right hand, it was covered in shallow red scars. She noticed his gaze. "Sharp talons," she laughed, "my glove came off! By the way, I'm Antonietta Cristaldi, I run the place. What can I do for you anyway?" she said as she set down the small percolator and cups. "Well," said Marco, "have you had any birds escape recently?"

She looked at him "Have you seen Bruno?" He looked bemused. "He's our Peregrine, he flew off two weeks ago. With all the cover round here it's difficult to get him back. Have you caught sight of him?"

"A client of mine said a pigeon was chased into her window, breaking it" Marco replied, "chased by a falcon." She looked concerned, "Are you a lawyer? You're not going to sue are you? We're on a tight budget here – we could not survive a big compensation claim, not now when I'm just getting on my feet."

She went on to explain her finances – a big loan from the bank seemed to be the basis. Marco studied her features. Small dark eyes, black shoulder length hair, a small red pert mouth.

"You see I'm totally committed to the birds and falconry. It's all I want to do." She got up and began pacing up and down.

"Perhaps I can talk to your client, avoid a court case, what do you think?" she appealed to him. "It's hard on your own, you know" she said "there's always something." She told him of how, out of the blue, the electricity bill had appeared, just when she least expected it. As he listened he began to understand that here was someone expert with the birds but a bit at sea with the finances.

"Perhaps you need a partner" he said innocently, "a business partner," he added, when she looked at him closely. "Can't afford it" she said "this place barely keeps me."

"Look" he said, "I can smooth things over with this client of mine and perhaps we can get her help to lure Bruno back – he must be living near her house – she has a bird table, perhaps the activity around it attracted him."

"Yes." she said enthusiastically.

Together they visited Pupella Spaccatini. Once placated, she was keen to help catch Bruno. It was difficult to get away but having extracted themselves from Ms Spaccattini's clutches, they set off back in Antonietta's green fiat. As she passed a local trattoria she said, seemingly spontaneously, "Lets eat." Marco realised he was famished. The food was excellent, local produce. They discussed birds, especially raptors, at length. After a few glasses of wine she said, "You know, you shouldn't be doing a stuffy city job – I can see your heart's in the country. You're really like one of my hawks, wild at heart but caged." She was looking at him in an intense way. "You did such a good job of sorting out my problem with Ms Spacattini, I think you should become my business partner, you've got the skills I lack."

Marco began to think. It would be a dream, working with birds, living in the countryside. He had always felt he was in the wrong niche. "Like a caged hawk" she'd said.

They left the trattoria laughing. "Forget the car." she said, guiding him towards a neat little house in the village. Unlocking the door she pushed him in.

_____

The next morning found Marco struggling to wake. Where was he? A note by the bed in a flowing hand read "Gone to feed the birds – back soon to make your breakfast." He began to recall last night. What had he said? Had he promised to become her business partner? Perhaps he did. Was there any way that could happen? – no, not in a practical sense he concluded regretfully.

She burst in the door. "You're still here - bueno." She bustled around heating croissants and coffee. They sat together quietly picking at the crumbs and sipping from the tiny cups. "I'd like to be your business partner" he said, "but I don't have any money, so I'm going to say I cannot really do this."

"*Cretino*", she exclaimed, "I don't need your money! I only gave you that story of being broke because I thought you were a lawyer. I've got loads – no, what I need is you, your body of course, and your business brains. We could run the Falconry together!"

Back at Avaro the staff never really found out the whole story. The patio door claim came in, approved, but Marco didn't return. His letter said he needed time out and had resigned.

Avaro management accepted his resignation and the office work swept over the crack that had once been his place in the company.

_____

Antonietta knew a wild hawk cannot be coerced and only becomes accustomed to being kept by patience, regular fresh food and plenty of outdoor exercise on the lure. Eventually the bird is ready to fly free, returning to its owner at command.

Marco was naively unaware of his mate's understanding of him. He only knew that it felt right between them, and that when darkness fell and he alighted on her gloved hand, she would talk to him in low tones, and sensuously stroke his golden feathers.

TALKING WITH ELFGIFU

The 5.03 from Euston took 43 minutes. As usual it was crowded and he had to stand. He resented that. He'd paid for a seat – how often over the past five years had he got one? By Tring they were thinning out and he sat down at last. The irony was he'd been sitting all day almost, at the computer, and tonight, well, apart from walking the dog, he'd be in front of the telly.

He glanced at his paper – pictures and a headline of the Iraq war, the crisis in Darfur, identity cards – he couldn't take it in. Media saturation, compassion fatigue, he had it all – so did most colleagues of his age. The teenies and early twenty somethings were too busy on the social scene of clubs, pubs and restaurants to be worried by the headlines. It was when you were settled with a wife and kids that you became a media victim.

Tonight in the remaining minutes of the journey to Leighton Buzzard he began to fantasize of escape from the grip of the media.

His wife was not at home yet from her job and for another hour on Mondays the two kids were still at her sister's till seven. Scout the dog as ever was keen to see him. What was it like for the dog? It could sit out the back in the yard, but it was a long lonely day without the pack, from 8.30 when the kids left for school until he got back at half six.

With the lead on, they made their way up to Lowe Park Wood. Steve liked it here – ancient trees, brambles growing in wild tangle, the smell of the earth. The dog raced ahead. James had called him Scout because he said the dog was finding the way like an Indian scout.

"Why had things got like this?" he mused. "I mean this lifestyle – no fresh air, sat down all day, hardly seeing the family, the dog not happy?"

Several of the trees were like old friends- he had given them personalities. The kids laughed when he told them this chestnut was Arnfinn the Wise and this beech he called Elfgifu the Emerald Princess.

In the summer light she did seem like a princess to him – the sun slanting through her small soft downy green leaves dappling the glade in an emerald glow. The names came to him from his half course in Anglo Saxon at university. That time seemed a world away – the freedom! Not only the time freedom but the freedom to think. Here with the trees, fixed and ancient, his mind felt calmed but more complex as if, while here, it grew creative roots and branches.

Was it possible to change, not just jobs – he'd done that – no, change everything so he didn't have to commute, so he got up later, saw his kids off to school and had, not just more time with Eva his wife but more time when they talked and laughed – like when they first met.

As Steve walked down the forest path he thought about being a forester but a friend had told him that it was all time pressured and profit squeezed like so much these days. He wouldn't have liked cutting the trees anyway.

Trouble was he was earning quite well and with his wife's wage they were quite comfortable or were they? Financially yes, but they were paying a terrible price in lifestyle. Could anyone escape except the rich?

He tried to think this through logically. He wanted change. He knew what he had now was what he wanted to escape from. Being an accountant he resolved to do a mini audit then and there in the wood. Taking out a pen from his suit pocket ((he still had it on on bar wellies and a waxed jacket) he listed on the left the things he hated and on the other side the things he craved.

Commuting	No commuting
Extra long hours linked to above	shorter flexible hours
Sedentary work place	moving about a bit

Low family contact time	more family contact
Constant pressure	less pressure
Time split up - no flow	flow
Snatched pleasure	pleasure spread in work and leisure
dog unhappy	dog happy

Well there it was – he'd at last written it down. Far from being gloomy he felt better, he knew the enemy. Armed with this knowledge he could plan a campaign.

On the train back on Tuesday he started to compile a list of jobs that might fit the desired criteria of the audit – thatcher, ornamental blacksmith, saddler, potter, running kennels, falconry, writer, but he found he dried up quickly.

That night he explained the criteria to the kids and asked them to come up with some ideas. Out came explorer, actor, photographer, dog breeder, zookeeper, sailing instructor (because James his son liked boats) and horse riding instructor and farrier (because his daughter liked horses).

When his wife came in she joined in the game and added family baker, gardener, fish farmer and running a B&B. The game petered out when James had to go to Karate class and Sally's friend turned up.

As she ate her reheated pizza, Eva looked across the table at Steve. "Are you really thinking of changing jobs?" Steve considered her mood. She seemed relaxed enough for what he had to say, sometimes that was not always the case these days.

"I would like to change everything." She looked at him thunderstruck. "So you've met another woman?"

Steve sighed inwardly, why did women always assume this? "No, definitely not. I mean everything, but you." She looked relieved but still apprehensive. He must have rambled on for an hour about his audit, his feelings about their life. She watched him quietly then burst into tears. "Oh no," he thought, "I've blown it," but she came and put her arms around him and said "It's how I've felt too – squeezed – squeezed emotionally, squeezed on time. I would love it if we could change it all, but how?"

"Well, we've taken a big step just identifying the problem and coming to an agreement," he said. "That sounds like work speak" said Eva. "What you learn at work can be useful in the rest of your life you know", he said. She laughed " I'll make some coffee, then we can discuss it further."

Now they had re-established a common goal they felt closer and later, lying in bed, they talked into the night.

"We've got a lot of value in the house", he mused. "Even after we pay the mortgage?" she queried. "Yes," he answered "it's gone up a lot, but we need income."

"Isn't part of the problem that we think we need so much that we've locked ourselves into this lifestyle." She said.

"Maybe, but it's more than that" said Steve "We're both working for organisations that are driving us all the time, looking for best value, as you said, squeezing us – so much so that in the evenings we're just to tired too do any thing but sit passively in front of the telly and be depressed by the news."

"How drastic does this move have to be, couldn't we stay here and do different things?" said Eva, but Steve was already asleep.

Eva worked as a nurse – she loved nursing but the bureaucracy was getting worse – targets, forms; patient care was being buried under paper. She had resigned herself to soldiering on aware that work was making her short tempered. Steve's ideas had made her begin to think she could give it up.

No seriously new ideas came to Steve as the train rattled home on Wednesday but on Thursday, as the train moved through the countryside, he saw the canal.

He recalled there was an old canal side boatyard for sale. They offered secure moorings, a shop for boat owners, a slip for boat repairs. There was also a workshop for engine work but the gem was the house – with work, he thought, it would make a lovely B&B.

The canal made him think of his Dad. His father had loved the countryside but had ended up in an engineering firm, a bit like himself, trapped really. Dad had walked along that canal with him many a time in the evening, and they'd fished together from the bank on weekends. He recalled the beauty of the canal in different seasons, the autumn days, the surface misty and ethereal, then, in a hard frost the canal rigid and white. By spring, swollen with melt water and rain, a slow current moved the surface. Summer heat, still and drowsy, brought dragonflies hovering over its surface and ducks squabbling in the reeds.

It was like that when he took Eva to see the property with the estate agent on Saturday. He was apprehensive, but the canal shimmered and worked its watery magic. The place did look run down, but there were cheerful window boxes, tubs of geraniums and an air of practical purpose. They listened as the estate agent outlined the potential not only to earn from the B&B, but also from the several other businesses. The man in the workshop explained that he rented it from the current owner, as did the lady in the shop. Three or four brightly coloured boats paid regular mooring fees at the site and on the slip in the boatyard, the owners of a narrow boat were finishing off the decorative paintwork of her cabin. They all stopped to chat.

Taking a short walk along the towpath together, Eva turned to Steve and, embracing him, said "yes, lets do it, there's so much... energy here, the right sort of energy."

Using the increased value of their present house as security Steve got a mortgage on the canal property. That way they could stay where they were during the renovations. They sold up their old home as the canal house was finished and began the B&B soon after. They were working together, they were still close to the children's schools and there was no commuting. It was hard work and new work but Steve and Eva were happy. They were back and forth to suppliers, chatting to the guests, the boat owners and the men in the boatyard and workshop, as well as doing the cooking and cleaning.

As for the dog, he was happy — he had a massive pack now. He could sit in the yard with the men or go with Steve in the van. Somebody always wanted to walk him along the canal in the morning, as well as lunchtime, and Steve still took him to Lowe Park wood in the evening. The dog noticed another thing too. No one seemed to watch television very much now, especially the news – they were all too...well, active.

JADE (YU)*

She had been staying over at Kirstie's house. They'd been mucking about with her mum's cosmetics in the bedroom. When she got home the next day the old bubbly Jade seemed to disappear. Her body language changed. She began to look down instead of straight at people.

Her P3 teacher, Mrs Findlay, sensing something was troubling her became more attentive, asking her how she was feeling, how was her mum and dad? How was the gerbil? But Jade seemed distant.

At the parents night, Mrs Findlay relayed her fears to Jade's parents, Jean and Jack Mackenzie. Mrs Mackenzie said she'd been quiet at home since she'd fallen out with Kirstie, her best friend.

That night, Jean talked to her daughter. She asked Jade if she was feeling ok, was there something troubling her at school? "No school was fine" replied Jade. "And Kirstie, you never go to see her now." Jade slid silently under the covers.

"It'll be the holidays soon," said her mum encouragingly "We're going to uncle David's." Jade liked uncle David's – it was a large farm in the Borders with sheep and cattle, hens and and even a couple of ponies.

On holiday, Jade seemed to pick up. Uncle David and Auntie Meg had a son called Joe, who was fun. He was always into wild games played out in the fields and woodland. Auntie Meg, dark and slim, filled the role of a typical farmers wife, but she also painted and the house had paintings everywhere with little sculptures on the window sills and on the sideboard.

Meg was walking through the hall when she saw Jade standing by the mahogany side board holding one of her sculptures – small, valuable, special... Meg checked the inner voice that wanted to say "put that down," Something in the way Jade handled it, carefully, studying it closely, made her hold back.

"It's from China" said Meg "from the Ch'ing dynasty – it's made of a precious stone called Jade."

"The girl looked up at her. "Like my name?" she asked. "Exactly," said Meg "Jade is a very precious stone in China, I expect that's why your parents called you that – your name means precious jewel."

"Is it always this sort of slatey green?" asked Jade. "Well, different shades were used for different types of object. This is an especially good piece – it's very hard to carve." continued Meg.

Jade carefully put down the piece and ran off.

Meg stood for a moment. There was another side to Jade this year, she seemed deep, sensitive, with an awakening artistic curiosity.

The encounter with Jade had revived old memories. Meg had been given the sculpture fifteen years ago by a man she had fallen deeply in love with when she was a student. He had told her the green jade statue was of Kwan Yin, representing unconditional love for all beings. Her time with him was a magical time. What would life have been like if she had married him? Best not to dig these things over now, she mused, as she bustled out into the kitchen garden.

Jade was feeding the chickens with some bits of bread.

Meg called her over and asked if she would like to help her pull some veg and prepare the meal. As they worked, Jade asked some more questions about the sculpture. Did Meg have any other things like it?

"After dinner" said Meg "I'll bring out my secret box and we'll look at it together."

While the others washed up, Meg and Jade went upstairs to the bedroom.

From the top of the big walnut wardrobe Meg lifted down a red lacquered box with brightly coloured birds painted on it. The lid was held shut by a red ribbon tied round a cloth button.

Meg opened it carefully. Inside, the box was lined with matt black paper. Jade sensed that this was some secret part of Meg's life that she, Jade, was being let into.

There were several things in the box. Meg took out a long paint brush and a stone rectangle with a well cut in it. "This is for Chinese writing, they do it with a brush, see, here is the ink block." She fished out a black hard block, looking like a lump of liquorice. "I'll show you later how to do it."

She then took out two little brass cymbals tied together on a string. "These are for temple ceremonies." They clanged together and vibrated with a clear sharp sound.

She took out a tiny grey clay temple about the size of a large thimble – it had a pagoda roof which curled up at the ends.

Meg unfurled a piece of cloth "this is a black ink painting on silk." It felt light and filmy, unlike anything Jade had ever seen before. In the foreground was a gnarled pine tree, then in the middle ground, a portion of the great wall with a waterfall close by, then in the distance, a mountain. "You see, the Chinese style doesn't have any perspective." said Meg. Jade was intrigued. Meg explained "in the west – that's here, perspective became very important – you have a focal point, with lines running to it." She pointed to a painting on her wall "like that," Jade glanced up, – "the Chinese didn't see it that way but their paintings are beautiful in their own right."

Meg now took out a small green box. In it was something that looked like a collection of tiny mummies. Little shapes wrapped in green silk and tied with red ribbon.

"What are these?" said Jade. "This," said Meg with a flourish, "is the Chinese orchestra."

Jade stared in fascination as Meg took out each little parcel and laid it on the downie. She carefully unwrapped each piece.

Little porcelain figures emerged of girls, their black hair up in elaborate coiffures. They were clad in long flowing embroidered robes with loose sleeves. One was sitting cross legged with a flat string instrument across her knees, another knelt holding a tambourine. Three others sat on round seats, one playing cymbals, one playing a lute and the other holding a black lacquered clapper.

Jade stared dumbstruck. They had her eyes. Each had eyes exactly like her own.

"Aren't they beautiful?" said Meg.

Jade thought back to the fateful day at Kirstie's house when Kirstie, painting on eyeliner, said ,"you've got funny eyes."

Jade had looked in the mirror – first at her eyes then at Kirstie's, then her own again, back and forth. Her eyes were different from Kirstie's… Back home Jade had looked at her parents' eyes. They were like Kirstie's not like hers.

Next day at Inverlochy Primary School, Jade had looked round and realised no one in the class had eyes like her – all the girls had round eyes, mostly blue.

Aunt Meg gave her a poke "Hello, are you still with me?" Jade looked down.

All that was left in the box now was a thin black book, like a sort of wallet.

"What's that?" said Jade sensing a slight hesitation in her aunt. "It's a photograph album." she said lifting it out and undoing the faded blue ribbons. Meg let out a sigh "This is me and Ming Chen at the Heaven Gate. I was very much in love with him." Jade stared. A man dressed casually in jeans and a shirt stared back. He had the same eyes as her. "This is Ming Chen and I with friends at the university." Aunt Meg's voice faded as photo after photo of Ming Chen and other people were laid by the orchestra, photos of people with her eyes.

Jade said "Are there many people in China?" "Over a billion. It's a big country – the most ancient and accomplished civilisation in history," said Aunt Meg emphatically.

"Why do I have eyes like those people?" said Jade quietly. "Why? It's because you're from there." Meg knew that Jade had been told she was adopted but she sensed perhaps that was all she had been told. "My sister and your father couldn't have a child so they..... adopted you. I was able to help because, through Ming Chen, I had many Chinese contacts." Jade was listening intently, "You were adopted from China." As Aunt Meg talked on Jade's mind drifted off. So, she didn't have funny eyes – she was Chinese – billions of people had eyes like her – beautiful people.

When they went downstairs, Jade found Joe and disappeared off into the fields to play.

For the rest of the holiday and beyond, Jade seemed transformed, happy, joyous, with a light heart, because.... because she knew her eyes were beautiful, she was beautiful, like the ladies of the Chinese orchestra.

*YU is the Chinese word for Jade. In China, while a symbol of love and wisdom, Jade is also said to act as a sort of communicating device, linking us physically and spiritually to our world on both the earthly and heavenly plane.

Some believe also that handling Jade allows its properties to be absorbed by the body.

P3 is the class for 7/8 year olds in Scotland.

HOUSE, TREE, PERSON

It was Ludmilla's housewarming party and they were playing the house, tree, person test. It's a sort of psychological thing where you each draw a house, a tree and a person. Some, usually self-appointed, guru in the group interprets the results.

In most cases the guru hasn't really a clue to your inner psychological world and the whole thing is pretty shallow – used mostly to get people talking and arguing, which doesn't take long after a few vodkas.

When Dimitri drew a boat there were cries of "foul! – that's not allowed, it must be a house."

"You can live in a boat" Dimitri countered. They grudgingly agreed but said "Well, where's your tree then?" He quickly sketched in a potted plant on the deck. The person was himself, of course, at the wheel.

The self-appointed guru, Ludmilla, said, "I think Dimitri wants to sail away! The boat means he can up anchor at any time." "No" said Alexei, "he's just anti-social, he doesn't want to live in the city with the rest of us."

"Hey that's rich coming from you," said Dimitri "what's this castle you've drawn with battlements and a moat? I think you want to keep out the working classes."

Ludmilla's friend, Marika had drawn a small wooden dacha, the kind you see in the country. "Look," said Dimitri, "here is someone with humble aspirations."

"Class has nothing to do with it." said Marika. "I like the woods and the countryside. I want to leave the city, grow flowers and vegetables, and sit by a wood burning stove at night."

"Any room for me?" said Alexei. "I won't be lonely," said Marika "not like you in your big castle. I'll have my animals, a dog a cat and my hairy Grishka."

Grishka was Marika's boyfriend, absent tonight because he was attending a weightlifting competition in Minsk. "Ah," said Alexei "who can compete with the hairy Grishka indeed?!"

Ludmilla strangely had not drawn her new home, a swish flat in the Nerinsky district of St Petersburg, but we shall return to her drawing later. She was peering at the minute drawing of Boris Spensky, a friend from work. "What is it Boris?" she squeaked. "A library," he said gruffly. Boris Spensky spoke little and was usually useless at parties; he often just sat watching people in astonishment, thinking, "How do they do it? I mean, converse on such trivialities," or he was buried in a book. He would bring his own or on arrival, immediately find one in his host's bookshelves.

"You can't live in a library," said Ludmilla. "Why not?" Said Dimitri.

"Because where would you eat and sleep?" she replied.

"I'd have a camp bed and a spirit stove." said Boris. "You need someone to look after you" said Marika, then she added mischievously "a big castle would house all your books and have rooms to spare, eh Alexei?"

Dimitri giggled, the thought of Boris and Alexei living together as a couple seemed so ridiculous.

"What have you drawn Ludmilla?" said Marika. Ludmilla unfolded her piece of paper. Although she was now sitting in her nice new flat with its trendy furniture she had drawn a tent, a large one, a palm tree and a camel.

"But that's not a house" said Marika. "Yes it is – people live like that all the time," replied Ludmilla indignantly.

"So you want heat" said Alexei "Our Russian climate is too much for you?"

"I am fed up with the freezing winters," said Ludmilla, "I want to be warm."

"I don't see a person, is the camel you?" said Marika playfully. "I'm in the tent, lounging on large cushions" said Ludmilla. "Not on your own I bet," said Alexei.

"The camel belongs to my lover, a sheikh, who has just crossed the desert to visit me, and me alone." They all looked at Ludmilla. The fantasy was a revelation. Ludmilla seemed so plain and well, sort of uninteresting really and now, this.

Suddenly looking up from his book, Boris looked at Ludmilla and said. "Is it a bactrian camel or a dromedary?"

Marika, Alexei, Dimitri and even Ludmilla burst out laughing.

"To you, money is something to be hoarded after being sought. You can exchange it for material things. To me it is part of a mechanism. I am the natural force of intuitive growth, bestowal and disbursement."

Mulla Nasrudin

THE HOARD

It was a strange paradox — as Fergus grew richer he became more and more concerned about losing his money. He found himself worrying if his investments were sound — were those shares likely to go down?

What if property took a dive? He began to buy paintings — old masters, as an investment — it seemed they never went down in price, but the downside was they were a target for theft. He spent increasing amounts on security at his various properties.

When share prices did crash he managed to come out of it — but badly shaken. A property dip left him more worried. He made a momentous decision — he converted all his wealth into gold — it was the only thing he felt was reliable, it even looked like wealth and he could touch it, feel it.

As the bars began arriving by armoured car at one of his residences — one that was unoccupied — he was always there to greet them and supervise the storage.

He was no fool. He knew that the driver and his mate were fully aware of the contents of each case on a delivery, so he always had them leave the case in an empty room so they did not see the others. He varied the armoured car companies so that the driver and mate did not repeat a delivery.

In fact he kept the whole thing so secret that his family did not know nor did his friends.

He felt more and more secure as the gold, now stacked lovingly by himself in the cellar, piled up.

He found his world shrinking – he no longer had to visit his broker or talk to estate agents – he had no real need for the world of commerce which he had been so immersed in.

He found it difficult to go away for any length of time from the house for worrying about his gold – was it safe? He had the only keys to the several locks that were in place.

The years went by. He lived simply off an allowance that an aunt had left him. He spent little. He found himself one day elderly. The government, whom he'd never trusted, sent him a pension! Then they assessed him as being below a certain income level and gave him more, plus a winter heating allowance. He even got a rebate on his council tax. If only they knew.

As time went on he began to worry about who he would leave his gold to. He did not respect his few relatives – they had all rather shunned him as he grew older and more eccentric. He had let it be known years ago that he had lost all his wealth in the Stock Exchange crash.

He needed someone who would understand – someone who liked gold and knew that you really had to keep it safe, to look after it.

When he broke his hip he was out in the driveway of the house – the postman found him and called the ambulance.

Hospital was a frightening place at first – lights – noise – so many people coming and going. Fairly quickly they operated on him and had him back in the ward. He asked about the cost – there was none – it was free, the medical care, the meals, everything. The nurses were kind and attentive, the doctors efficient. Who was paying for all this? When he asked they said, "You are, out of tax." Fergus had not paid tax for a long time and even when he had, he had tax lawyers trying to minimise it.

He began to feel something he'd never felt – he felt held, supported, cared for unconditionally. The staff were giving of themselves everyday to people like him and those with more serious conditions.

He asked to see the hospital administrator. He told her he was thinking of giving a donation. "What did it cost to run a hospital like this?"

"£340 million a year," she said.

Fergus was aghast – "Where did all that money come from?" he asked incredulously.

"Each and every person gives so much a month from their pay towards it – when you have millions of people you get large sums." she replied.

Fergus realised two things – first his gold was doing nothing, nothing good, and secondly, it was not a powerful sum. Sure it was a lot but nothing compared with the power of all these people giving a little each.

"Donations can be useful," said the administrator, guessing that Fergus's enthusiasm was waning. "We need a new scanner, that will cost us £1.5m. We have a campaign to raise the money." She went on to explain what the scanner was for and how many people would benefit from it.

Fergus was taken home by ambulance and to his surprise was met by a physiotherapist and the district nurse. They settled him in and then a social worker appeared. She arranged for a carer to come in to cook him a meal and do a little cleaning.

The next day Fergus asked his lawyer to call. He instructed the lawyer to transfer the gold to the bank. He re-invested his money in stocks and shares and property. He made a donation to the hospital plus he redirected some of his earnings to give them a yearly donation. He employed a cleaner and a cook, thus easing the burden on the local care service. Most of all he did not avoid tax, and when he paid it he paid willingly. And indeed it was as well he felt that way, for by the time that the Inland Revenue claimed the tax unpaid for the last twenty years on his "gold store", and the Social Security had claimed the means tested benefits back – his fortune had somewhat dwindled.

When he did pass away he died happy knowing that Inheritance Tax would take another chunk of the remainder. He left everything else to his cook and cleaner, knowing that they would spend it quite quickly. When his lawyer objected to this at the will writing, Fergus said "I made a great mistake in my life. I misunderstood money – it's really like a fertiliser – kept in the farmyard it's no good. It must be spread out on the fields to help things grow."

KEEPERS OF THE FOREST

"Dermot, your tea's ready." It was his wife calling from the kitchen.

He was about to start on a new set when he discovered he was low on wood. There was a little piece of African blackwood but all the ebony was gone on the last set. He was pleased about them – they played beautifully. They'd gone to Australia poor things. The heat, what would it do to them? Still at least the chap could play. Uillean pipes are sensitive to humidity. They might be alright. Where was it they went? Brisbane, it was humid there, subtropical the chap had said.

"Dermot" the call came again. This time he heeded it and went through to the kitchen. His workshop, a converted garage, was right next to the kitchen. Handy in some ways but it meant you were a little too accessible.

"You planning another set?", said Niave his wife. "It's the wood, I've run short." he replied.

"You know" said Niave who was a primary teacher, "my class are doing the rainforest right now and these tropical hardwoods you use are from the rainforest." "So?" He said.

"Well they take a long time to grow especially that African Blackwood and Ebony and that Brazilian mahogany."

Dermot sighed. His wife often saw a moral issue in the everyday things of life.

"But Niave. You see, they're the best for the pipes. African Blackwood gives a good crisp sound and Ebony, well it gives a little softer, mellower tone."

"What will you do when there's none left?" she retorted — and another thing each tree supports lots of other creatures, insects, birds, frogs."

"Frogs! Get away."

"Tree frogs" she replied.

"I'm going round to mum's for a minute" she said after they'd had their tea. "Ok" said Dermot, but she was gone already out the door.

Her school folder lay on the wooden kitchen table. It was a ring binder and had a large yellow plastic cover. The letters Rainforest Project were boldly printed on the front. Dermot picked it up idly. He flicked it open. There was a loose page of kids' stickers each lettered "Keepers of the Forest" — he put these aside. Then a diagram entitled rainforest ecosystem explained how life was mostly in the canopy where the sun was. Monkeys, parrots, sloths, eagles, insects. She was right, there were a lot of animals up there. The trees grew tall in competition and because of the high rainfall not because of the soil — it was poor.

He turned the page. A scene of devastation. A huge swathe of forest cut down, burning branches, huge logs being carted off. The text explained how this was a complete loss of habitat for all the creatures. They were homeless or killed in the process. The soil then was swept away by the rain. Pictures of huge gullies and canyons on the next page underscored the point. Careful selective logging in a sustainable way and using alternatives was the way forward it said. Overall, the rainforests were being logged so fast that global climate was being affected...

"Ah, so you're getting the message," said Niave returning.

"Just having a peek. What does it mean?" he asked, "when it says global climate change could result."

"Well you see it's a wonderful thing the rainforest, it encourages the very rain clouds to form that make it grow — it's a complete system that brings water and life together in a continuous cycle. If the trees were to go you'd get something like the Sahara, just desert and rocks."

"Wow," he breathed "but how am I going to make pipes?"

"Use alternatives." said Niave. "What did they use before we discovered the Amazon?"

True what did they use? He was a relatively young pipe maker, 27, just starting out really. He had always been using blackwood or ebony and mahogany, even right through his apprenticeship with Padraig Crowley.

Dermot phoned Padraig. His former "master" was 70 now but still making. "Sure" said Padraig, "Box is your man. Years ago I made a few out of Box."

"How's it for tone?", enquired Dermot. "Well it's softer toned than ebony, sweet, very nice. You know I might have some on the wood pile, I'll call you back."

Padraig's woodpile was in fact a barn with a very well organised selection of timber, all neatly stacked on spacers to allow the air to circulate. The timber had to be seasoned to let all movement out of it. Few pipe makers seasoned their timber these days. Woods like ebony and African Blackwood didn't move much, but if Padraig had got his box "green" i.e. new cut, he would have stacked it in the pile.

Later that afternoon Padraig called, "right at the back, sure the label reads 1990, it'll be fine now. Are you thinking of trying it?" Dermot thought for a moment, it would keep Niave happy and, well she did have a point. "I cut it meself," continued Padraig "it's from the Comeragh Mountains right here in county Waterford. Nice colour, yellowish. It's fairly scarce, slow grower you see." Dermot knew his old master – he certainly wouldn't be giving it away. At last they agreed a price and Dermot drove over to collect it that afternoon.

The drive from Cork to Dungarvan took him two hours. Padraig was bright as ever. Dermot always marvelled at Padraig's "woodpile". It took years to build up such a stock. It paid off because you bought wood at today's prices and made at a future price – wood was always going up in value. Padraig had taught him that – it was getting scarcer and scarcer.

Dermot wondered what Padraig's take on the rainforest thing would be.

"I could see it coming" he said "the quality now is not so good – its right, you cannot go on just taking, you have to give back. Come and see this."

At the back of Padraig's cottage was a bit of hill land surrounded by a drystone dyke. Rows of little trees about a foot high stood green and bonny in the sun.

"Buxus Semperivens" said Padraig. When Dermot looked puzzled, Dermot continued, "the latin; Box." You see we're on limestone here, that's what they like, but they're slow growers and long livers – it'll not likely be me that'll be getting the use of them."

Dermot was humbled and once again struck by the skill of his master. Not only had he laid by wood for the future he was now growing his own, not for himself, but for his art, for his pupils, pupils like Dermot. He always learned something from Padraig.

On the drive back he gloried in the green fields and hedgerows – green because Ireland got a lot of rain.

Niave was surprised when he talked to her about buying a small plot of land outside Ballynock up the coast. She was even more surprised and quietly pleased when he told her what he wanted to do with it. "You see, I understand now" he said "in a way we are all keepers of the forest."

The Box Tree
Box in the wood
Where the foxes pad and play
Wood in the Box
Hard and yellow
Makes a sound, warm and mellow
Under the pipers elbow.

MINIMALIST HEAVEN

There was a plop in the water beside the houseboat – a spent rocket stick. The fireworks continued to blaze away, magnificent bursts and showers of light, heralding in 2005. They seemed to go higher and brighter each time. "How do you end a firework display?" she once asked at a party – "with darkness" came the smart reply, but she meant it got you to such a high that you felt terribly let down when it ended.

Some people were like that in your life – lots of fireworks then when they left, gloom.

Light was so important in people – the spark of life. Well <u>he</u> might have gone but he left a spark of life behind him, Jason. Her boy was nearly ten now, standing quietly beside her watching the arcing rockets.

The houseboat was like all boats, neat. No, not cramped, but neat. If you put things away it was liveable. It had lots of clever little cupboards, and storage places.

The furniture was mostly built-in except for the deck chairs. Here they really were deck chairs. On sunny days she could sit out in one and work on the after deck.

That's where they were now, on the after deck in the shadow of a larger boat that they moored against on the lower Thames.

The houseboat was cheaper than a flat and more fun. Jason had whooped with delight when she mentioned it. The river was never boring, always busy with other boats and wildlife. Even tonight, in the half dark, she'd seen swans gliding across the reflections on the water.

Jason had loads of friends at school – the houseboat made sure of that. They came aboard with such glee. Adults were different. Some all stuffy and sniffy, worried about safety and space. Others found it delightful. It was a sort of weeder outer of friends really.

She turned back towards the warm glow of the cabin. "I'll stay out a little longer mum." "OK, darling," she replied. It was well after midnight now, time for cocoa and some toast. Despite its smallness, she liked cooking on the boat. Minimalist, someone had once called her at college. "If they could see me now," she laughed. It was true – she did severely question the current society. How much stuff did you need for God's sake?

Some women she knew had umpteen dresses and coats, racks and racks, two or three cars, rooms of furniture.

She liked to keep life simple. Once when she was travelling with a huge backpack she met an Australian girl. All this girl had was a credit card, the clothes she stood up in, a spare pair of knickers, and a spare sock. The girl explained that every night she washed one pair of knickers and one of the socks she'd worn that day. This girl had covered thousands of miles like this – a modern aborigine on walkabout.

It <u>was</u> a battle – to reduce your life, to keep things at bay. She thought of jumble sales she had run at college to raise funds. All that junk, and then there were the hoarders, attics full of clothes. She heard of one woman who had drawers and drawers of unused linen. She kept all the children's clothes even from when they were babies. Another county family she knew kept every edition of their weekly paper in the attic. "The ceiling will come down one day," they gaily said, proud of their hoard.

On the boat, even if you wanted to you couldn't do that – there just wasn't the space.

A white shape appeared in the doorway – "Lightbox" the cat had returned from a wander ashore. Jason, his hair glistening with raindrops re-entered the cabin. "I want to design firework shows, mum." "Why not?" she said, handing him a mug of cocoa.

The tiny crew of "The Minimalist" were reassembled.

THE GREENLAND PROPHECY

Alana was packing her bags. "Off again are we?" said Livia her flatmate "Yes," said Alana, "Scotland, photo shoot for country casuals." "Lucky you" said Livia "I never seem to get out of London."

"Well, it'll probably be cold and there'll be midges," replied Alana. "That reminds me - insect repellent." As a model, Alana had to be prepared for the most appalling conditions. A photo shoot could demand one to be scantily clad, naked even, frolicking in the winter sea and smiling. The public had no idea of how tough it was. Starving oneself, constantly preening, changing your hair, walking correctly. True it had been exciting for about a year and then well, it was a job. You couldn't relax, eat like a pig, get sunburn or trip over and crack an ankle, otherwise you didn't work. And there was always the competition – hundreds of younger girls were pressing all the time to take your place, so you didn't complain, took the jobs when you got them in case the agency didn't ring again.

There *was* the travel. Alana had been all over Europe, to the USA and even Greenland for the Vodka shoot. Usually you didn't have time for sightseeing but in Greenland of all places, she got stuck with the camera crew because the plane broke down. Four whole extra days, in brilliant weather admittedly. They had amused themselves as much as one can in Greenland – a skidoo trip, an outing on the fjord in a kind of leather boat and a visit to the fortune teller's hut.

Each of the crew, Patrick, Jo and Lucia and Alana had gone into the hut one at a time to have their fortune told by an old Inuit lady. There was a lot of joking and joshing. Alana had been told her spirit was a bird spirit, restless, always in flight,

She would only find peace when she met her opposite spirit - it was tall and green with arms sticking out at right angles.

"Sounds like a TV aerial" said Lucia waspishly. Jo the camera man had said "I know what it is she's describing – a tree! Of course, the old crone's never seen one." It was true, Greenland was treeless.

At the time Alana had thought the old woman's assessment of her was pretty accurate. She was restless and always flitting about even when work did not demand it. What did the rest of the prophecy mean? Should she live in the woods?

Back in London, busy schedules pushed the Greenland incident from her mind. And now this Scottish shoot.

It was raining at Inverness airport when the plane touched down. The shoot crew were experienced and knew that a few drinks and some good food would lift their spirits, set them up for tomorrow.

The camera shoot was of country casual skirts, some of them tweeds and other fabrics with autumn colours. They were to meet someone in the bar from Scottish Nature Conservation to guide them to locations where the heather was in bloom and where there was other vegetation which would give contrasting hues to the garments.

Alana was between relationships. In truth she was glad of the break.

In her mind she classified men into Lions and Swans. She'd been out with a Lion recently. Lions tended to be bossy, unfaithful and short tempered but did look magnificent. That had been Cato, Afro Caribbean, very good looking but she'd dumped him when she found out he was double dating her. Before Cato was Alec; now he was a Swan, faithful, slender and beautifully caring. She had dumped him too but for different reasons. He was too perfect – beside him she felt flawed.

Now for the moment she was happy to be uninvolved, but she did wonder if there were any other "creature types" out there that she might be compatible with.

The crew tumbled into the Highland Hotel. Leaving the camera gear in the foyer with the receptionist they headed to the lounge bar. Sitting by himself was a tall dark haired man with a tanned complexion. He was nursing a half pint.

Jo broke the ice. "Are you the guy from SNC?" "Yes I'm Donald Mclaren their field botanist," he said holding out a hand.

"A plant man then" said Lucia the soundwoman. Donald's voice was slow as if he wasn't used to talking to people a lot, he seemed to search for the words. "Well anything that's not animal such as sedges, trees, heather, bushes, flowers, that sort of thing." His light highland speech intrigued Lucia who found accents so fascinating she had tapes of them at home.

By now Jo had ordered drinks and put then on the tab. At the table, Patrick, the team leader, produced swatches of fabric and shade cards. Laying them out, he asked Donald about the location of suitable vegetation for backdrops to the shoots. Pointing to the shade cards he said "We ideally want these sort of colours in the back ground."

Donald spread out a map and pointed to several possible locations, marking them with a pencil. "Here there is heather and bracken. That will give you purples and browns. Over here are Scots pine – they have a lovely bronze bark and dark green needles, while over here is Sitka spruce, a lighter emerald green. For the greys we should go down to the river, there you've got river boulders and river gravel against the pines."

"Sounds great, but its all weather dependant of course" said Patrick gloomily.

"But I've checked the forecast, its good for tomorrow" said Donald confidently.

During this conversation Alana was studying Donald over her gin and tonic. Quite the handsome chap. Steady, quiet, but sure of himself.

The backs of his hands were tanned like his face – he obviously spent a lot of time outdoors. She'd never met a botanist before. Her men had all been from the media or the city.

At dinner she sat on one side of him, Lucia on the other. A sort of rivalry for his attention was between them.

He had a habit of explaining things by drawing little illustrations on napkins. She had asked about the difference between Scots pine and Sitka spruce and by way of explanation, he had drawn the needles and cones of each in detail, quickly and skilfully.

He wasn't married or engaged – Lucia had got that out of him. He looked like the sort who would be married to his work; not a flit about type – no, he was firmly rooted like one of his pines.

I bet he's full of old fashioned male chauvinist ideas thought Alana. To test this theory out she shifted the conversation ground onto women's rights, but to her surprise, Donald felt women should be totally free, not tied down to the home, free to work and that couples should share the childrearing. She found herself slightly disappointed. Had she secretly wanted to be swept off her feet by a hairy highlander with caveman attitudes? Donald was so liberal he probably didn't hold on to most women.

Donald for his part had been interested in her but he felt she was a bird of passage, a city girl. He did not for one minute believe he could be of interest to her so he concealed his feelings.

Alana, used to men falling at her feet worked all the harder to get Donald's attention only to find him, well, appearing indifferent.

The next day in the minibus the shoot crew followed Donald's car to various sites. Sure enough the vegetation was as he had described it. The weather was sharp but sunny and the shoots went well – so much so that after two days they had it all wrapped up.

Finding out that Donald did wildlife paintings, Alana had asked to see them. He picked her up at seven on the last evening and they drove back to his place. It was wooden, not in a log cabiny sort of way, but a modern Scandinavian house, set back in the pinewoods near a small loch. She was intrigued. Here was this gorgeous man living on his own without apparently needing a woman. She praised his drawings and paintings, evidence of his finer feelings. He had cooked supper – over the meal with several glasses of wine he asked her about her world and her work. She got a little sloshed and rambled on about things. She fell asleep in the big armchair by the woodburning stove.

When she woke it was late morning. She was lying in Donald's bed. He wasn't there. She peeked in the living room. Under a blanket on the sofa was something breathing. A pair of feet clad in outdoor woolly socks, stuck out over the armrest.

She looked at her watch. Drat – the crew were off by plane today at eleven. Using her mobile she dialled Patrick. He was very forgiving "We'll cancel your flight luv" he said. "You make your own way back."

She stayed the next night – this time they both shared the large wooden bed, but work meant she had to leave the next day.

At the airport she hugged him and said she'd be back next weekend. "I'll be here" he replied. As she walked through into airport security she looked round at him standing there in his green fleece. He smiled and held his arms straight out mimicking a plane.

She suddenly remembered the Greenlandic woman's prophecy "Her opposite spirit would be tall and green with arms sticking out at right angles."

A tree, of course! Donald was no Lion, or Swan; he was a tree, solid stable, dependable, static, ideal for her. She was a pigeon, restless, flighty, migratory, with him she could flit in and out to roost. Would this analogy go as far as nesting?

"My boyfriend is a tree," she murmured as she boarded the plane. She giggled at the concept, wait till Livia heard this.

BODY BALANCE

Inga quickly changed for her body balance class. She valued this class. She felt it was keeping her figure and keeping her supple.

It was Thursday; Kim Loden was the instructor today. There was a rota – Tuesdays; Sophie Fotheringhame, Wednesdays; Lin Chan, on Thursday; Kim. During term time Inga could only manage on Tuesday and Thursday.

The class met in the new sports centre. Contrary to her husband's male fantasy, the women who attended were a variety of shapes and ages. Nor were they clad in pink single piece lycra. Instead the women appeared in grey or blue tops, stretch trousers, bare feet.

Kim Loden had been a kick boxer someone said. That explained her tight lithe muscular body and rapid movements. She wore a stars and stripes top with red spangly trousers. After the warm up, the pace was fierce. Kim had once explained her philosophy to the group "in my class you'll <u>know</u> that you're burning off all those chocolate biscuits and pieces of cake."

Into the routine, the women all moving in unison. Yet there was always one, sometimes two, who moved left when the others moved right. Movement dyslexics, thought Inga, a primary teacher. In the spirit of inclusiveness no one said anything even the instructor.

You became familiar with peoples bottoms as they stretched and even wobbled in front of you. There wasn't the regular spaced breathing of athletes – there were sighs, sharp intakes of air and even groans. In at least one routine there was the audible crack of unwilling bones.

Interspersed between the aerobic bits were the stretching exercises. These had curious names until you did them. The eagle, the triangle, the sheep. With all this shaking about there was one bodily function that was being suppressed by many of the women. Indeed the whole session became a meditation exercise to not let it out, but the Frog tested even the best meditators. In the Frog you crouched like a frog your hands flat on the floor your hind legs bent and your bottom in the air. Then you flexed and arched your back so your bottom was raised and lowered in the process. This always proved too much for someone. Occasionally delicate, sometimes not, the sound sang out amongst the heavy breathing and the groans. Inga felt it difficult not to laugh.

It was different on Tuesdays, so different that some missed out Kim's Thursday class with its slight air of masochism.

On Tuesdays Sophie Fotheringhame set a more ethereal tone. Sophie had been ballet trained before taking up aerobics. She was tall and fair, not particularly slim now after having three children. Her loose brown silk top was offset by her stretch yellow trousers. From slow warm up exercises the class then moved into elegant limb movements, a sort of Burmese dancing complete with facial expressions. The session always ended with each woman putting her hands together in a prayer posture and Sophie would pay homage to the goddess by saying "Namaste". At first few of them said it but it felt quite nice to say it together so now they all joined in.

Inga had never been to the Wednesday class until today. It was the school holidays and her husband was watching the kids. Although Lin Chan was probably about twenty-eight, she was small, and moved with a natural grace. She was dark and very slim. She had the body of a child, thought Inga. Lin wore a loose blue wrap over jacket and loose trousers, while on her feet were small blue embroidered slippers. When Lin spoke her not quite perfect English made them listen attentively.

Her routine appeared at first like one long warm up – slow studied movements carefully choreographed, using arms and legs. Inga soon found that it was as demanding as the other sessions. It required strength, it left you energised as the other exercise did, but somehow without sweating or getting out of breath.

All the exercise classes are so different thought Inga as she towelled off after the shower. It was nice to have the variety. Kim's class when you had been overindulging, Sophie's class when you needed to feel in touch with your feminine side and Lin's class when you wanted to feel strong.

Really her husband hadn't a clue what her body balance classes meant to her. Well he did in a way – he said she was always in a better mood when she came back.

STRIP OF LIGHT

He noticed it the third night. In the past two weeks he had got into a habit of going out for a drink at nine and not returning till one or two in the morning. Worse for drink he'd stagger up the stairs and along the corridor. The first few nights he hadn't noticed in the gloom of the passage. Then on the third night he saw the yellow light under the door of room seven. Over the following nights it was always there, that warm yellow strip.

He drank because he was alone. He went to the pub for company. He'd not always been alone. A broken relationship lay behind him like a shipwreck on a reef. He'd made the beach but he could still see the wreck from the shore, that's what made him drink.

In the daytime work distracted him. He wasn't lonely then. At work he was fun, lively – but inwardly he dreaded the end of the day. His workmates all seemed to have families, wives, girlfriends. The flat was empty, bare. Only his stuff. If he left the dishes they awaited his return. The unmade bed a symbol of hurried departure, not welcome return. Each of these things underscored his loneliness. And so he drank, he went to the pub to meet people, but found he was often already drunk when the pub filled up. Then he bought drinks overgenerously and people avoided him.

He staggered up the stairs looking at number seven. There it was, the yellow strip. Intent on eying it, he tripped on the carpet and sprawled full length. From the floor he was level with the strip. He could see a table leg, a foot, a man's foot. Somehow he was disappointed. He wanted to see a woman's ankle, feminine warmth. He felt cheated by the yellow light.

The door opened. A man's hand, strong and powerful pulled him to his feet. "A bit worse for wear, eh?" The face that confronted him was lean, weatherbeaten framed by close cropped greying hair. He let himself be guided into the room. It was plain, sparsely furnished. He had not only hoped it was a woman who occupied number seven but somehow that it would be comfortable, big sofas, welcoming. He was sat down. Coffee was made.

"I'm Duncan" said his rescuer as he was handed coffee.

"I've heard you come in every night." he said.

"And I've seen your yellow strip." replied Jake.

"My what?" said Duncan.

"Your yellow strip below the door".

"Ah, the light." said Duncan.

Jake noticed the table was covered with plans, rolled out like charts and weighted at each end. An angle poise lamp illuminated the details. Duncan followed his gaze.

"My next project." he said. Jake dimly perceived these plans were for a boat, a big boat.

"I've been working on her for the last few weeks – burning the midnight oil."

Jake was sobering up.

"What do you do for a living?" enquired Duncan.

"Mechanic." replied Jake, now feeling shivery and tired.

Duncan explained about the engines – Detroit Diesels, 1000 horsepower. Jake's mind engaged, engines, that meant something to him. They talked engines for an hour. Back in his own room finally, Jake crawled into bed. He felt relaxed, comfortable. He fell into a deep sleep.

Saturdays were normally maintenance days, the launderette, a few bits of shopping. He usually woke about 11am, especially if the previous night's drinking had been hard.

Today his door was banging. A voice, Duncan's, calling him. Something about the boatyard. Yes he remembered he'd agreed to go with Duncan to the boatyard to see the boat. Without washing he slid into last night's clothes and opened the door. "Ready" he croaked.

They clattered down and out of the flats to Duncan's truck and roared off.

Jake felt both a little stunned at this early departure, but also a little exhilarated.

The bright sun made him screw his eyes up.

The truck wove through the busy harbour area to a collection of large sheds and stopped.

"Harry's Boatyard" it said in faded white lettering on a large corrugated hangar. They entered through a tiny door. A smell of wood, tar and oil assaulted Jake's nostrils.

"There she is" said Duncan, with pride. "The plans turned into reality, nearly finished – just some rails and fittings and the engines to go in."

Jake was captivated. With the boatbuilder they went into the office. Over coffee Jake found himself engrossed in the discussion, then again as they toured the boat. "You like her?" said Duncan. "She's fantastic" said Jake.

Alone in the master's cabin Duncan turned to him.

"We're going to run this baby out to the Azores and do whale watching tours." Jake's eyes widened. "I need a mechanic but a sober one."

Jake looked at his feet then up again. "I'm not an alcoholic."

"I know" said Duncan. "I can tell because I once nearly was – off it now, never touch it - but if you go on" he said to Jake "you could become one." Jake's eyes widened. "What started you on the benders?" said Duncan.

Jake opened up about his marriage, the lack of children, how it all just crumpled.

Duncan looked away from Jake out of the cabin porthole then he said

"When she left me my wife said it was because it was too hard to compete with the ocean." He paused "You know, some say that "woman" is the most powerful force in the world. In the main I would say that analysis is right, but for people like me" he went on "she has a rival, the sea... I've thought about this a lot. When I'm at sea I can feel safe, supported, like with a mother, but the sea is also like a lover, exciting, feisty, fickle, as well as smooth and gentle. Sailors still like women but almost as a distraction – the sea meets their deepest emotional needs, she is their main love."

When they launched the Sea Witch, Jake moved in and lived aboard. She had spacious cabins, showers, a spanking new galley. And afloat? He did feel curiously at home – safe and supported. Moreover, in the coming months he grew to love the sea's many moods.

And his drinking? It didn't stop altogether but it trickled down to something he was in control of.

A few months later if you had looked inside his cabin late at night, you would have seen him pouring over the paper work for his seagoing engineer's ticket, and from the outside, in the companionway, all you would see was a strip of yellow light along the bottom of the cabin door.

A PLACE TO WORK

The *cheka cheka* of the cicadas grated out over the long limp afternoon. No wind riffled the dry beating heat to give relief. "Stridulation, yes, that was it," she thought, remembering the term for the insects' behaviour. By the end of the summer, she had heard, that the little nobbly bits they rubbed together on their legs were quite rasped away. "I can believe it," she mused, as the sound continued. "Any musician would get worn down with that much work."

She wondered about their ears.

Mercifully, at dusk, they ceased – by then she was indoors preparing a salad for herself, a misticanza, wild mint, wild rocket, wild fennel, garlic and lettuce – each single taste like a clear note against the others.

It was still hot but the sting of direct sunlight had gone – the thick house walls and terrace tiles gave back gently the heat they had collected so fiercely during the day.

She sat out again with a glass of wine feeling the warmth on her legs. She touched the terrace wall – it felt smooth, glowing and alive, the temperature of skin.

From the town below came the sounds of muffled voices, laughter then footsteps echoing in the paved narrow streets. Siesta was over. She could start work.

At night, when it was cooler, human energy emerged renewed. During the day it evaporated away with the heat. For the cicadas it seemed the other way round – perhaps they needed the heat to make their sound or maybe, just maybe, they knew nothing else would be moving, making a sound to compete with them during the heat of the day. "Ecco", they had it all to themselves.

She found now she could only work here in Istia. The island was so small there were few cars. Traffic noise, such a problem at home, was minimal here. Most people walked everywhere in the little town, even the old.

To compose you needed to hear the voices of the instruments in your head.

Back in Kent there were planes flying over to Heathrow, trains on the high speed link and the ocean roar of motorway traffic that never abated, even at night.

Yet she needed sounds as inspiration – but they had to be distinct, not muddled together or masked in a fog of white noise.

Here the sound of one bird, the Scops owl, had inspired her deeply. It had a sound like a single church bell ringing. When she first heard it at night, it made her think of a small chapel, a solitary saint ringing out from his campanile over the olive groves.

A soft wind forced the huddled umbrella pines in her garden into an ancient wispering.

The town gave up its sounds to her at night. Sometimes in the early evening the trill of a singer trapped like a canary in a nearby apartment would rise up like a soul released and float over the roof tops.

She once followed a couples' argument clearly through four movements; *allegro, vivace, presto, prestissimo,* then all fell tantalisingly silent.

Had they made up or were they sulking in separate rooms?

Here the shops were discreet – no piped music tried to lure you siren like from the street. Only human cadences prevailed in cafes or bars.

The whole island seemed to talk to itself. Natural sounds including the voice had not been surpressed by the invented machinery of mankind.

She took up her pencil and began to form a phrase, hearing the notes clearly in her mind.

THE RUBBISH MAN

Fred Skelton had worked for Putney District Council for 30 years. He was a bin man or, in the new speak, a garbage disposal technician. He liked his job, well at least for the first 20 years, then under the Tory government, his work had been "outsourced".

He now did the same job for a sort of privatised quango – the pay was a little less, and the conditions a lot worse, more hours for one thing and they seemed to want the rubbish collected at high speed. He'd never understood that. Rubbish collecting wasn't a race, where was the urgency? In the old days you had time for a chat with the kitchen porters, the housewives, shop owners. Nowadays you were so pushed you hardly had time to nod, and at xmas, well, they didn't know you, so why should they give you a prezzy on your last collection? "Nah it wasn't the same."

Fred lived alone in a nice little council house in the borough of Putney – he'd bought it when his mum still lived with him, God rest her soul. A neat little front garden, a few roses and a patch of green. Out back, a lawn, a border plus a little shed for the tools. He was a clean and tidy sort, thanks to mum, and he could cook, after a fashion, nothing fancy – he still did himself a roast on Sundays.

He'd noticed that the street was changing – new people moving in – people carriers, BMW's, husbands and wives both working. They did up their houses.

His was beginning to stand out – no major facelifts, same old windows and doors – no garage, he didn't own a car, although he could drive.

He was still fit and active for 47 — yes, he'd started with the council at 17 — seemed a steady job then.

The job kept you fit — lifting and heaving. Fred did go out — to the pub, and he went on holiday — usually to his aunt, mum's sister in Brighton, for holidays.

The mates at work kept chivvying him about this — "Why not try a foreign holiday? They're so cheap even a skinflint like you could do it!"

He was lifting the bins outside a travel shop when he saw in the window a holiday billed as a last minute bargain, in Spain, and the price was incredibly low. The dates just matched his 2 week break. He thought, "I'll show em." After the shift finished, he went back to the travel shop and booked. Later he phoned his aunt and told her he'd be down for a weekend but this year he was off abroad for the his main holidays. She seemed relieved.

He bought a Spanish guide book and studied it in detail. He followed the tips closely. Sunblock, light clothing but he wondered about the food.

He spoke to old Mrs Johnston about the house as usual — he'd be away for two weeks but this time he was going abroad. She seemed suitably impressed, "Spain eh, you'll be going to that place Ibitcha won't ya! All them gels" Fred didn't quite catch her drift till later as he sat with his inflight drink flicking his way through a holiday magazine. It had an article on Ibiza. Well he wasn't going there. Unfortunately, as there seemed to be a lot of semi-naked lovelies leaping around outside night clubs. No, his destination was a small fishing village called Porta Cruz. With little knowledge of Spain, he had not really studied his destination that carefully — it was a bargain after all.

As he stepped off the plane the warm air surrounded him in a pleasant embrace. He felt relaxed at once. The small airport whisked the passengers through and onto their bus. As it was dark, Fred saw mostly lights, with palm trees lit up exotically from below. At the hotel, check in was a blur as the crowd was dispersed to rooms.

On holiday Fred liked to lie in late – he figured as someone who was up everyday for a 6am start that he deserved this luxury.

Consequently he missed breakfast so found himself outside the hotel mooching down the street looking for a cafe. All he seemed to see were bars. One caught his eye – The London Bar, all day English Breakfast. "That's more like it" he thought, and went in. Although the place was very Spanish in decor, the lady behind the bar greeted him in a strong north country accent.

As Fred worked his way slowly through his full English breakfast, the bar seemed to fill up with regulars – as he found out, they were all expats – people from England living out here all the time.

He got chatting. When in answer to their query he told them he was on holiday, they said "you should come out here permanent mate – great climate, cheap booze and lots of lovely women."

Fred replied that someone in his job was unlikely to be able to afford it. They fell silent, then one of the men said "Where'd you say you're house was?" Fred explained the location again and, yes it was his, no mortgage. Well, said the man, it's probably worth…. and he named a huge sum. "You could easily buy a place here." "Oh," said Fred, letting this thought sink in. Leave Putney?

Back at the hotel a little sozzled, he crashed out for the whole afternoon during what the expats had told him was siesta time. He awoke about five and lay on his bed watching the dappled light from the slatted blinds play on the wall. Fred began to day dream. The English chaps at the bar seemed pretty savvy about property – was his house worth that much? It was funny, the same lot that had outsourced his job and cut his wages had made him property wealthy by letting him buy the council house. Could he do as was suggested, sell up and move? It'd mean giving up a steady job but the job wasn't what it was. If he spent all the value of his current house on a property out here he would have nothing to live on. Also, if it was valuable now, wouldn't it just keep going up in value if he kept it. What if he wanted to keep it and maybe buy something out here. Someone had tried to explain how to do that last night.

He spent a few boozy nights in the English bar while mortgages and second mortgages were explained to him.

He returned home all fired up and right away went to see a building society that specialised in this sort of thing.

They said they would process his application in a few days.

Back on his rounds, Fred worked with a renewed vigour that attracted the notice of his mates, but he kept his plans to himself.

Outside a Spanish restaurant in Devon St., one he'd "picked up" from umpteen times, he suddenly asked one of the kitchen porters "Hey, I've just been to Spain – it's fantastic – why are you fellahs here when its so nice there?"

"No jobs," shouted the porter from the door.

Fred took the bin back. "What's your name", "Juan", said the porter. "Look," said Fred "I am thinking of buying a house there, could you help me? Fill me in on some details – we could meet for a drink."

"Si Si." said Juan.

At the Dog and Whistle, Juan with his red wine and Fred with his pint, they discussed Spain. Fred learned that jobs were tough to get in certain areas and Juan and a lot of his mates came to the UK, Germany and France for jobs. Where do you stay when you're here?" said Fred. "Flats," replied Juan "no good places."

"Look" said Fred, a thought crystallising in his mind, "I've got a whole house, would you and one of you mates like to rent a room?" Juan was cautious, but agreed to come along to Fred's next night at eight.

Fred opened the door the next evening to see Juan and a pretty girl standing there. "This is my mate Carmella." said Juan. Fred realised that 'mate' had been lost in the translation. However what difference did it make? He showed them the room, the biggest in the house, with a view over the back garden. Carmella was delighted – their current flat was small, dirty and looked over the railway. He asked them to set the price and was astonished at how much they expected to pay. He felt it was so much he reduced it a little.

Life with Juan and Carmella gradually altered Fred's domain – the food, the music, the sounds of Spanish being spoken.

Fred discovered that Juan and Carmella worked incredibly long hours – they were saving to go back to Spain to open a bakery – Juan was a qualified baker. Carmella explained they needed about £100,000 to set up – they'd saved £30,000.

These conversations set Fred thinking. He couldn't see himself in Spain just sitting on a terrace drinking wine or playing golf like so many expats – but he could see himself working – doing something.

"What if I put up some of the money?" said Fred during one of these conversations. Juan looked at Carmella "How much Fred?"

"If I sell this place," he replied, "I could make up the difference, say £70,000."

"And in return?" said Carmella.

"I need to work" said Fred "so you employ me – driving, cleaning up, that sort of thing. I'll have enough left over from this sale to buy a house of my own."

So, twelve months later, Fred had sold his house and moved to Spain. He found himself a spacious flat and worked for the bakery, gradually doing more and more deliveries as his Spanish improved. With his bakery wage and the pension he got from Putney District Council, his income was at least as much as before. Like a real Spaniard, in the afternoons he had a siesta. In the warm evenings, he went to a bar. Because of his rounds he got to know a lot of people and there was always someone to chat with.

Life went by at an easy pace. He had one or two of his mates over to stay – they would arrive pale and exausted and go home restored. They were envious of his lifestyle. At his old work things were, if anything, worse now. "The company just treated us, well, like rubbish." said his mates. Fred ordered another round.

THE RED FIDDLE

The reddish varnish had a deep warm hue with a certain translucency. The rest of the fiddle seemed unremarkable. The scroll was roughly cut, the peg box a little too wide, the f holes seemed positively jaunty and the purfling was only drawn on. Mr McMaster looked up, "I'll give you £50 for it" he said, "is there a case too?" The young man left the front room for a second and came back with a wooden body shaped violin case.

David was clearing out his aunt's house. He'd advertised the fiddle in the local paper "full sized fiddle and bow for sale, offers."

McMaster had been the first to reply. David had not known his great aunt had a fiddle or whether she had ever played. He'd found it in the attic at the back of some books. When she died she was an old lady, 93. David was twenty five – he had always thought of her as old. He had met her a few times as a child but more recently he'd been in Edinburgh as a student and she had let him have a room. He was a quiet type given over to reading and Radio Four. He went out to the occasional play or concert.

"Is that your best offer?" said David. "It is" replied McMaster, "It's not worth more."

David knew nothing about fiddles except that at the concerts he went to they produced beautiful music and the players held them with care, love even. McMaster didn't handle the fiddle with love. David declined the offer.

Duncan McMaster walked huffily down the stairs of the tenement flat and out into the street. "Everybody thinks they've got a bloody Stradivarius" he mused as he bent into the easterly wind. He could have sold it for at least double. "Ach well. There'll be others."

Over the next few days several people called about the instrument. Mrs Laurie found it too big when the child she brought with her couldn't reach the fingerboard properly. A rather haughty Mrs Sneddon made several derogatory remarks about it, voicing the thoughts out loud that McMaster had kept to himself. A Frederick Isaacs, who called, said he was a repairer; wanted it so he could cannibalise it for repairs to other fiddles. He did at least praise the varnish, "quite exceptional" he had remarked.

David hadn't felt right about any of them.

Responses to a repeat advert the following week brought no-one until on Friday a rather breathless girl rang to see if the violin was still available. When she heard it was, she arranged to come round at 5 that evening. Answering the door, David found a striking redhead with shoulder length hair dressed in a long black dress and black waist length jacket. She strode in boldly and seeing the open fiddle case lifted the fiddle straight out. She tightened the bow and then began to tune the strings. David stood by transfixed, such energy, such purpose. She was the first one to even think of playing it. She began to play, warm up execises, stopping to adjust the strings here and there. Then she launched into a piece of music he was familiar with. She seemed lost in the piece, a picture of concentration. She suddenly stopped and looked at her watch. "Fine," she said, "How much?" David had if anything over the last few days become less keen to just part with the fiddle. "Why do you want it?" he asked. The question seemed to throw her. "Look," she said looking at her watch again, "I haven't got time to haggle. The neck of my own instrument came loose during practice this morning and I need an instrument for a concert I'm doing in an hours time." He looked at her keenly; she was vibrating with pent up energy. Her eyes shone and her red hair had a tone not unlike the varnish of the fiddle. He was surprised at his boldness when he said "Here is the deal – I lend you the fiddle and I also get to come to your concert." She seemed to see him for the first time. She calmly looked him over, carefully, as if he was a new piece of music, before she replied, "I need to go over my performance. Since we are now both going to the concert I will rehearse here."

With that she launched into her pieces for the concert. David sat down. Her presence and the sound of the violin filled the room.

LEAVING THE TREES

Yura moved slowly back to the jeep. His Mongolian assistant, Oyon, said "dhuruv", (four). "Da" (yes) muttered Yura. They were studying Bactrian camels in the desert scrublands south of Saynshand on the edge of the Gobi.

Last night the temperature was down to -5° and the morning air was still cold. Yura was still amazed by Oyon's eyesight – without binoculars she could see, not only for miles, but pick out individual animals against the landscape.

The Bactrian camel was tough and had thick hair to insulate it against the low temperatures.

In winter, temperatures can fall as low as -50° and heavy snow can fall, covering the open steppe; the heavy frost gives it an icy shield – grazing animals cannot dig through to the grass beneath. Mongolians call it the "dzud." Here, near the Gobi, they were beginning to see how well adapted the camels were. Browsing off shrubs as well as the grass, they could survive when the ground was covered.

The researchers had been warm enough last night; Oyon had made sure of that. In their round tent, a deep felt floor covering, thick sleeping bags and on top, a heavy felt throw had kept them warm. Oyon was a young Mongolian woman attached to the State Nature organisation, a tiny unit of the Tourism Department.

Apart from some minerals and its pastoralism, Mongolia had little wealth except incredible scenery – mountains, deserts, rivers and the wildlife. The government wanted to earn foreign currency by attracting tourists and had set up nature reserves to that end.

Yura was on a six month visit, his second from Moscow University Zoology Dept. Bactrian camels were the subject of his thesis. His home was near Tobol'sk in Siberia, hundreds of miles north of here – a place of dense coniferous forests.

On his first visit to Mongolia he had missed trees immensely – the smell of pine needles and the aroma of wood smoke. He missed the forest animals, deer, bears and capercaillie. He felt exposed on the Mongolian plain – from some of the hills you could see, and be seen, for miles across a landscape of sandy coloured dunes or waving steppe grassland.

Oyon drove the jeep at speed back to their camp, kicking up a trail of dust. She was mad for speed. She rode the same way, always fast, breakneck.

She had almost grown up on horseback. Her parents were sheepherders still living the traditional way out on the steppe. Oyon had studied and made it to university – she was good at science but she loved nature and being outside – zoology had been an obvious choice for her.

Yura marvelled at her practicality. She could mend jeeps, fix radios, look after horses and cook. Admittedly a limited menu, mostly variations on mutton, but still.

"Would you like some buuz (mutton dumplings)?" asked Oyon, getting out the cooking pot and gas stove. It was still chilly, buuz would be warming. "Of course." said Yura.

"Boris seems to have got himself some company," he continued. "Yes, he's popular with the ladies" said Oyon, "but he's got a temper with the young males." Boris was a magnificent male Bactrian with a dark shaggy neck mane.

As the buuz heated, Oyon wrote up her morning's field notes.

Yura liked buuz – his mother made dumplings at home and as a Russian he was not averse to meat, but here it could be meat for breakfast, dinner and tea. They even had dried meat with them at this camp. When he had looked at it suspiciously Oyon had told him that this was what Ghengis Khan and his hordes had lived on as they conquered the central plains of Asia and beyond. Obviously Oyon's implication was that if it was good enough for great warriors it was good enough for Yura. He didn't complain – Mongols were not tolerant of whingers. Their life was tough and fussiness was not understood. Yesterday they had a camel stew from meat a herder had given them. It was surprisingly tasty with the herbs Oyon had added.

He watched her now, small and neat as she stirred the pot. She had beautiful eyes and a ready smile. Her skin was lightly tanned by the wind and sun; around her slim neck she wore a necklace of wavy metal strips alternating with small bells.

She was good company, telling him magical Mongol tales of spirits and demons that seemed almost sacrilegious to his secular scientific mind.

But this had not been the only challenge. When Yura first arrived, his fieldwork approach had been conditioned by his own professor's approach and the forest. He had studied lemmings at undergraduate level. The approach was impersonal i.e. you looked at lemmings as a population fluctuating up and down, you looked at their place in the food chain – in essence they were objects.

The method Oyon had been trained in was pioneered by English biologist Niko Tinbergen and his students, such as Iain Douglas Hamilton. You distinguished the individual animals in a group using a combination of photography and drawing and then followed the behaviour of the animals using these visual identifiers, sometimes adding radio collars.

Oyon was a skilled observer and she was able to pick out the individual camels they were studying with ease.

Yura was quietly converted to this method in a very short time, but he realised also his earlier training had been blocking his view of nature. These new methods made you think of the animal as a being with a life and a personality.

Back in Moscow another thing was different — with the collapse of communism as an ideal, people were scrabbling for some spiritual pole to cling to — the orthodox church, or spiritualism or American born again baptism. Here there did not seem to be the need. The earth and the sky were so big your spiritual mind grew on its own, it didn't need an 'ism' as a crutch as it limped along in the material world. It was as if, back home, the trees had blocked his view of life, had set lines round his existence.

At first in Mongolia he missed the trees, now on his second visit he was glad to shrug off their confinement and return to the openness — to let his mind roam freely across the steppe.

Oyon said she was a Buddhist, but Mongolian Buddhism had this curious shamanistic element that linked it strongly to the environment. The prayer flags at their camp fluttered messages and paid homage to the ever present wind.

Buddhists here had reverence for the landscape, for sacred lakes and for sacred mountains.

As a zoologist he understood their concept of impermanence, of things in a constant motion of becoming, changing from state (Bardo) to state. Birth, growth, adulthood, parenting and death states were familiar ground to a zoologist as well as the thriftiness of nature in recycling biological molecules. Research had shown biological molecules do not decay on death but are recycled quickly into other living things and furthermore, DNA projected part of the biological self through offspring. So there was no physical death in that sense, but what of the spirit? Could the spirit survive the death of the host physical body and re-enter another?

The Shamans, he was told by Oyon, could make their own spirit leave the body in a trance and fly over the land to contact the spirit powers in order to seek knowledge, solve a problem or restore health and balance.

"Is it relevant today?" he had asked sceptically. Oyon said, "At present the human race is out of touch with mother Earth, father Heaven and the natural world. This is because we relate to them wrongly; by defacing and polluting nature we offend them greatly. The Shamans work to bring cleansing and healing to the earth and do ritual to restore the balance." When he had made some deprecating remarks she had snapped, "You're Russian, do you know what Stalin did here? – destroyed all the Buddhist monasteries, killed monks, suppressed Shamans – the sacred drum was forbidden, the spirits could not be called." "I'm sorry" he said, "it was before I was born. My own family suffered under Stalin. Why do you think I grew up in Siberia?"

She was staring into the fire. "I will say a prayer for a healing between us – both our families have suffered." She reached into her backpack and drew out some small branches of Juniper – she placed them on the fire.

She closed her eyes and began a low chant like a poem in Mongol.

When she stopped and opened her eyes he said, "can you translate for me?" She looked at him for a moment. "I will only tell you because you have told me that your spirit increasingly becomes pained when animals suffer or the environment is destroyed. The spirits are touching you. This poem will help you to touch them, to begin a dialogue." She began to recite, this time in Russian;

"Go into the morning sun on the river, into the reflections, the shimmer and the shadows, see the camel graze and the perching steppe eagle; he flies now, enter him and go into the wind. Melt into the rain and fall onto the ground, become absorbed into the body of the earth mother, flow from her back into the world."

Yura watched Oyon's eyes across the fire. She held his gaze. They were already close professionally but here was this new thing binding them together. Was this feeling his spirit blending with hers? She seemed to shimmer in the firelight. The metal strips and little bells on her necklace tinkled as she stood up and moved toward him.

THE BLUE CONTAINER

The croft door was open – a hen nonchalantly strolled out of it. Hector checked himself to let the hen pass. It gave him a quick look with a slight canting of its head.

The hen had upset his momentum. He had intended to boldly approach the door and knock on it, now, he noticed it lay half open, the inside in shadow.

He went closer – a faint droning sound could be heard – a sort of chanting.

He looked back down the track. He could see his car on the road, a glint of sunlight on the roof, the bonnet up.

His eye took in the rolling hill beyond, the green edging up to its heathery top.

It was a hot day. A bee flew by. He had calmed down a little – the walk had done it – up the track to get water. The radiator had gone again – he was half expecting it – he had some patching material but he needed water now to refill it.

The chanting had stopped. He suddenly became aware of that. He knocked on the part of the door in sunlight. Instead of an adult, a small child appeared – about six, dressed in a loose yellow summer frock that went down to her ankles – long plaited dark hair. She eyed him with interest "have you brought the plants?"

"Well, no" said Hector. "He's not got the plants" she yelled out to the interior.

"What have you got?" she asked. "A broken down car" he replied.

"Mum's got one of those" she said "I don't expect we'll need another."

The girl disappeared. She reappeared asking "What kind of car have you got? Because if it's a Citroen, Mum might be interested." "I'm afraid it's a Toyota" said Hector.

"It's a Toyota" the girl yelled back into the house.

"Look," said Hector "I need water for the radiator." The girl came out and crossed over to a little outhouse, bringing a blue plastic container. She began to fill it from a tap on the wall. The water pressure was low – it was going to take a while.

Hector sat down on a bench along by the door.

As he sat he realised how tired he was. He'd been driving since five from Edinburgh to get home to Skye for a funeral - his father's. Sitting like this it hit him again. All the way up he'd fought the feelings of emptiness and despair, of certainty falling away beneath your feet. His life had been going so well, his course, his friends. How could your life go from white to black just like that?

He sensed her watching him from the doorway. He turned. A young woman in jeans and loose green top watching him. She had a mane of long red hair, blue green eyes and a pale complexion. Around her neck was a string of black beads.

"Hallo, I'm Oona" she said with a smile – "You need water I see."

"Radiator" said Hector "on a Toyota – sorry no Citroen." Oona laughed, "Sometimes we get gypsies selling parts or dealing."

"Your're Irish" said Hector. "Yes" said Oona "from near Dublin."

"Would you like a cup of tea?" said Oona "that tap will take ages."

Hector realised he was tired and thirsty and, more than that, he needed to distract himself from his thoughts.

Oona reappeared with tea almost straightaway – "had just boiled some."

"No milk?" said Hector. "No, its Yogi tea – very Ayurvedic – it will restore you."

"Do I look like I need restoring?" he said. "Yes" said Oona.

"I'm going to a funeral" he said "my dad's." Oona listened – Hector let it all out. He didn't realise it, but he talked for about ten minutes about it all, how it happened, how he felt. While he talked, the little girl had set the blue container at his feet. As she looked up with her eyes into his, he sensed that she understood – she put her hand on his as he was finishing.

"This is Laksha" said Oona. "She is from Romania – an orphan, she knows about loss."

"How old was your father when he died?" said Laksha. "Seventy" said Hector, knowing as he said it that he had had a father's love for seventy years, something this little girl had never had.

The chicken came near, expecting in this gathering of people that a crumb might be in the offing. Laksha skipped off after the chicken.

"I was a nurse." said Oona "in Romania. We were just drawn to each other. I was also until then, a nun" said Oona "but I realised I wanted a child. I could give her a mother and a better life – so here we are."

"What was the chanting I heard before. "Oh" said Oona "I was a Buddhist nun. I'm still a Buddhist but not a nun."

"Buddhism," she continued "helps you not to cling to things, not to expect them to last, it teaches that every thing is impermanent."

The death of his father had made Hector aware of this with stunning clarity.

Sensing his interest, Oona went on. "Buddhism also teaches that everything is in a state of becoming, passing through different stages – it teaches that death is but a stage, an expected stage, on the way to rebirth in another form."

"So is my father?" said Hector. "Your father, and you, are becoming, changing into something else."

Hector semed lost in thought for a moment then picked up the blue container "Thanks for the water", "you're welcome" said Oona.

"I'd like to come back, you know, when everything is sorted at home, after the funeral and everything."

"Well, said Oona, "when you do, can you bring me a starter motor for a Citroen AX?"

As Hector walked down the track something had changed within. "Yes," he thought, "yes, the natural scheme of things is to be impermanent, changing, becoming." He poured the water into the radiator and restarted the car. He drove north more slowly, no longer at such a pitch of anxiety.

ILLEGAL

The minibus picked her up at 7 am. She and the others had been told by Costa not to form a group, not to stand together so as to draw attention – too many foreign looking people stood together might bring questions. So one stood in a shop doorway, another sat on the bus stop seat; she leant against the wall.

It was cold, her thin jacket ineffective against the biting wind from the North Sea.

The gang boss drove the minibus. He was always surly. Everything was a problem, people leaving, things breaking down. Was it all show so he could justify the pittance he paid them?

They were all illegals. Irena sat beside Ilona. They were both from Romania so they could at least chat without Costa understanding; he was Croat. Jaco, the third from her pick up point, was Russian from Odessa.

It would be cold today. Picking broccoli in January made your hands blue.

She barely glanced at the houses as they sped along. The wealth of the English. Their cars spoke of it, so many. Satellite dishes sprang like fungi from their neat homes. She burned to see inside, to see how they lived.

And how they drank. She was never out on a Saturday night but she heard them. She had been told to keep low, keep out of sight, stay in your accommodation. Costa rented them the ugly little flats in the back streets of Great Yarmouth. There they made what life they could. They worked so much that eating and sleeping was almost as far as it went. Someone had a radio, another might have some wine. They helped each other. Over all of this was the fear of discovery, deportation.

The boss kept talking about it. Step out of line and you're out.

"Was this a life?" Irena had often thought. This daily rhythm – the trip to the fields, a long day, cold often wet. What for? Going back meant failure and back to what? There were no jobs to be had. The village was empty now of young folk, all dispersed, like her, to the west or to the cities.

Here she at least caught glimpses of another life.

Some of the young women talked of marrying a Brit – that way you're in, all problems solved. A fantasy – the cycle of their days and weeks locked them in – they never met any young British men.

At the farm they collected on trailers and were tractored out to the fields. The ground was wet, slimy, so when the field workers got down their boots were soon clogged and heavy with thick clay. A drizzle had set in.

As she bent and stretched Irena recalled yesterday morning.

It had been bright and sunny.

A young man heading for the train station had smiled at her as she tried to look invisible. She regretted that. At home she would have smiled, flashed her eyelashes. She smiled now at the thought of it. Ilona caught her look saying "And what are you thinking of?" Irene laughed, "Guess."

"Men of course." replied Ilona, stooping to cut a stalk. "Of course." said Irena.

The gang boss couldn't stop them from dreaming.

Around them there was a mixture of men and women but Irena and Ilona had ruled out these men.

There were no prospects. These men had no money, no house, no citizenship. They were as likely to be shipped back as the girls, therefore the girls, being practical, dismissed them. Besides some of them were pretty rough.

The next day, while Irena was waiting for the minibus trying to look invisible, she looked up to find in front of her the young man who had smiled at her.

"My name is Colin." he said. She was confused. The boss had said to be invisible, there was danger everywhere – if you were found out… and there was Ilona and Jaco to think of.

She looked down again. Then up again.

"I'm guessing you're foreign." he said "Look here's my number." He handed her a card with an address and a telephone number "Perhaps we could go out together for a drink or a meal?" Irena was by now squirming. Part of her longed to do this, be normal, go out with this young man. The other part thought "I cannot, I am illegal. I have nothing to wear, only work clothes, no phone." He was gone when she looked up again. From her position at the bus stop Ilona gave her an inquisitory stare. Jaco across the street looked worried.

In the minibus Irena and Ilona talked of nothing else. He was handsome, dark haired, tallish and wore a long black coat that made him look sort of studenty.

That day Irena worked with a song in her heart. Somebody was interested in her. In her mind however, she was troubled. How could this progress? It was fraught with danger. The next day was a Saturday, launderette day. She and Ilona took their washing to the launderette – perhaps then? A coffee a chat, but to ring him?

At the break Ilona heard her out "It's risky, but there is a phone in the launderette." Usually Irena and Ilona were the only two illegals at the launderette – the others did all their own washing by hand to save money. Ilona and Irena had always used the launderette as an excuse to see a little of the outside world, to see what women here were wearing or rather, washing. Sometimes there were women's magazines – they looked at the pictures.

Irena plucked up the courage and rang the number. "Hi, Colin here." Irena's English was reasonable. She managed to get across that she could meet him for a coffee at a café opposite the launderette.

When she came off the phone the two girls chattered away, high on the prospects of this breakthrough. "Ask if he has a friend." said Ilona half seriously. The girls were giddy – the risks were high – but the dreariness of their lives made them hungry for excitement. The risks of the encounter added to the piquancy.

Colin was a bit puzzled. This girl was curiously coy. Not a trait he'd noticed in other girls in England. He was down from Scotland working on the large wind farm being constructed off Great Yarmouth Harbour.

Irena had attracted him partly because she had the looks of girls from his own area; slim, dark, slightly shy.

She noticed his different accent, got him talking about Inverness-shire, about home, so she didn't have to say very much. He was obviously smitten. When she said she had to go after forty minutes, the time of the complete cycle at the launderette, he was disappointed. A whole weekend stretched ahead of him. She made an excuse about strict parents.

When Colin set his mind on something he was never shy. "Look," he said, "take my mobile. I have another at work. That way we can speak and text each other." He thrust it into her hand as she rushed off.

Ilona was agog to hear all about the encounter.

She looked at the mobile in amazement. "He gave you this! He has been struck by the thunderbolt."

Back in Romania they say this when a person falls suddenly and deeply in love with someone at first sight.

Irena closed her eyes for a moment in excitement. "Phone him now." squeaked Ilona. Irena tapped in his number. Colin's voice answered, "Hallo, you're through to Colin Mackenzie at TKD, leave a message after the tone and I'll get back."

His Scottish voice was music to her ears. She left a breathless request for him not to phone her, only that she phone him. She would phone him back tonight.

And so a strange kind of love affair took off. Colin waiting for Irena to call – never able to call her. Fleeting meetings on Saturdays opposite the launderette. Colin had questions she couldn't answer. He did find out to his relief that she wasn't married, had no boyfriend. She clung to the story of over protective parents.

But Colin was no fool. He gradually pieced together a picture that led him to contact a friend who had married a girl from Peru. "Look" said Thorfinn, "even if she is illegal, as you suspect, she'll have to apply for entry from Romania – she'll have to go back, but you can go across and get married over there. Trouble is" said Thorfinn "she's probably got no papers at all, so when she tries to leave they'll pick her up."

"That's a problem, a big problem." thought Colin after he thanked Thorfinn.

He realised Irena was running risks by even seeing and contacting him.

He felt angry and frustrated. Irena might reject him because of her fears of deportation. She might even be in some kind of debt to a gang boss. She was so beautiful – he was entirely besotted; he wanted to take her out, to be with her, to take her home to see his parents even.

He began to worry about the details – there must be a way. False papers – he'd heard they could be bought. No, he didn't want to involve her or himself with the law.

What then?

He had two months leave due. He had been working solidly for four months without a break.

Costa felt something was up. He had an instinct for these things. He had been involved in crime since he was a kid. A key skill was awareness, noticing details. He had picked up the girls' change in behaviour – they were happy. Some boy had turned their head. He resented their happiness. His overboss was constantly on his back checking, making sure the money was coming in. Costa owed his overboss €50,000, the price for protection and safe transit to the UK. Until he paid it off he was well under his control. In turn, each of the people Costa had smuggled into the UK owed him €3,000. It would take them a long time to pay it back. It only worked because they were illegal – that way he had a hold on them, but likewise his boss had a hold on him. But Costa was used to this. He had gravitated to the Niko gang through working for various other petty crime lords – all used debt and violence to keep their henchmen in line.

First they got you in debt then they held a sharp knife over you. You lived in a state of constant tension, easier when the authorities were slack. Here they were closing in, getting tighter.

It was more and more difficult to work just with cash. In the UK, businesses that did, were targets for suspicion and scrutiny.

The gang were working in the fields as usual. Costa strode up to Irena and Ilona. "What have you two got to be happy about?" he said with a sneer, fixing Irena with his weasel like black eyes.

He didn't know the answer, they probably wouldn't tell him, not today anyway, but he wanted them to know he'd noticed something. Put a little pressure on, keep them in line. "Remember you owe me a lot of money."

When he'd left, Irena and Ilona worked on in stolid silence for a while until they were sure he was well away.

"Do you think he knows about the phone?" said Ilona.

"He doesn't know anything," said Irena, "He's trying to frighten us."

"Well we are already frightened" said Ilona "How much more frightened can we be?"

Irena didn't reply but she was thinking they could be much more frightened. Costa was accountable to no one but his bosses. He could get vicious even. She had seen him threaten one of the men with a knife in such a way that Irena was in no doubt that he knew how to use it. She would have to be careful, ever so careful.

Tomorrow was Saturday. She would see Colin.

Back at the lodgings the girls sat depressed, eating a stew, cursing Costa, the work, the threats. Ilona spoke. "My grandfather used to trap hares and foxes for fur. The animals usually survived if they stayed still but eventually my grandfather came along and killed them swiftly. If they struggled in the trap the jaws bit in, gave them pain, and they died through loss of blood. That's how I see our situation."

Irena said, "A fox will often chew its own leg off to escape. "True" said Ilona "he spoke of that happening."

When Colin met Irena that Saturday, she was white, drawn, ill looking. "What's the matter Irena? Are you ill?" She merely sighed and looked down. He had no idea of her situation. Colin told her about his time off – two months.

What could she do? She couldn't take time off. She told him she had to work – they wouldn't let her off. "Where do you work?" He asked. She looked at him. "In a shop" she found herself saying, "What shop?" "A shoe shop," she blurted out a name of one she had passed in the minibus – "Daltons, – as you leave the town."

"Can't you ask them? I could take you to Scotland."

Colin's leave started from Monday. Perhaps one day, she could be ill for one day. Sometimes people in the gang were too ill to work. "I'll ask off for Wednesday." "OK," said Colin "ring me."

Irena faked illness on Wednesday. She told Ilona what she was doing, asked her to cover for her.

But Ilona never got the chance. While Colin and Irena met in the café and then went for a drive in the fens, Immigration Officials struck at the farm. Costa and the work gang were surrounded and arrested, Ilona included – it was on the lunchtime news. Colin and Irena were in a pub talking when the TV in the corner mentioned the swoop. Irena was transfixed. There was the farm and Costa, then pictures of the work gang. Colin saw Ilona. "Isn't that your..." then he realised. She looked at him. He would abandon her now, turn her in. Tears were welling up in her eyes, for herself, for Ilona. Her friend would be returned to Romania, the debt unpaid. Costa's henchmen would be after their money. Ilona was going back to another hell.

Colin looked at her. "Are you like them?" he asked gently. She nodded. "I sort of knew." he said "Perhaps we can find a way through this – you see I love you, I brought you here today to tell you that and to ask you to marry me."

Irena's tears changed to tears of joy. She flung her arms around him. He kissed her, their first kiss – her whole being felt the kiss, and responded, like the parched earth, sighing, as it embraces summer rain. They were silent for a moment. She clung to him.

He whispered, "Do you say yes?"

"Yes, oh yes" she said.

His mind was racing. Immigration may have knowledge of Irena. "Your gang boss, will he split on you?" Irena shook her head. "No, I owe him money, I am an investment to him, better I should be free, that way he may get his money back."

"You owe him money?" She explained the system. How each level in the organisation owed a higher level money.

"How much do you owe?" "€3,000" she replied. "Wow," he murmured.

He realised he could pay this. He'd been about to buy a new car. He'd arranged a loan of £5,000 only last week. Instead of a new car he could buy her out.

"I have no papers," she said. "What, nothing?" said Colin.

"None, Costa kept them all, passport, ID, everything."

Yes, the problem of the papers. She was here in the UK but illegally. She could only apply from Romania to enter. They could get married but the rule still applied, she would have to go back to Romania to enter. She had no papers so as she left she would be arrested. Did that matter? She would be deported, a mark against her name – making it more difficult to enter a second time.

Colin looked at Irena, "For now you are free, you can come home with me." Not daring to go back to her lodgings, she allowed Colin to take her north in his car. She was stunned; was she really free? What of Ilona?

She missed her. She had no one to talk to about Colin's proposal. She had said yes but was it really possible?

That journey – when she looked back on it, seemed a dream.

English villages. English countryside then motorway, motorway, so many cars. Farther and farther north. The countryside changed. More hills, less trees; drystone walls replaced hedgerows; then on into Scotland. The landscape changed again, now from time to time pine trees edged the road, like at home.

They stopped in Edinburgh. "Tonight we are going to stay with Magnus, one of my friends," announced Colin.

Irena was exhausted by the day's events. When Magnus showed them a room she asked Colin if she could just sleep. "Of course" said Colin, "and tomorrow we shop."

Irena had spoken to Colin about clothes; all she had was what she had on. In truth she had little more at her old lodgings. Colin had told her how nice the shops are in Edinburgh but now she was completely physically shattered.

She marvelled at Magnus's modern bathroom. She stripped off and took a shower. The trials of the day washed off her. She had been through trauma like this before; the journey across Europe had been no picnic. In a truck, sleeping in barns, eating little. Then the boat, a small yacht – crammed in, then, Great Yarmouth.

At last here she was getting close to what she had come for. She fingered the stainless steel fittings of the shower and caressed herself with the fragrant body gel.

Over the last few days her love for Colin had made her forget that longing for material things that had driven her here. Could she have them and love? – it seemed too good to be true.

She slipped back into the bedroom. Between clean sheets in a clean room, nice, soft lighting, she closed her eyes and was soon fast asleep.

Colin sat in the kitchen with Magnus, an old friend from school and university.

"She's certainly a looker," said Magnus taking a drink from his can. "But" said Colin in a low tone, "She *is* illegal. I found that out today for sure." He told Magnus the story. Magnus studied him. He'd seen Colin with women before but never like this. He was intense, focussed, this had to be serious. "And you're taking her home?" "Yes," said Colin guardedly," Why?"

"It's just that, well, won't they ask a lot of questions?" countered Magnus.

"I'll say she's a student."

"OK, of what?" said Magnus. "Your mum's pretty inquisitive." Colin seemed to have forgotten that. He was so keen to show her off. What did he know about Irena – what had she done in Romania, what was her family situation? It dawned on Colin he hadn't a clue, just that she was beautiful and he loved her. "I'll think of something – going to take her shopping tomorrow." "You look knackered" said Magnus "and I've got work tomorrow. I'll leave you two lovebirds the key so you come and go." "Thanks" said Colin. He went off to bed.

Irena was absolutely out. They hadn't been really intimate, they hadn't slept together, they had only gazed at each other in a coffee bar and talked. In the soft light of the bed side lamp he watched her breathing. Her black hair spread over the pillow like dark silk, her lips slightly parted, her slender neck.

He remembered the fairy stories his mother had read him when he was little. It was as if one of them had come true – he had found a princess and he had spirited her away from the clutches of the evil king.

He could not believe her trust in him, her absolute trust – he suddenly felt very protective.

He put out the light and snuggled close, his arm around her.

And that was how they awoke at about 10 am. They had slept as if under a spell in the cocoon lovers make for themselves – the world magically kept at bay.

They awoke at the same time – surprised to find themselves together. They didn't go shopping that day. They didn't get up until 3.30 pm. but they were dressed just when Magnus returned. He guessed they hadn't made it out. "I know," he said "to hang with cooking, lets celebrate!" "Celebrate what?" said Colin. "Celebrate everything; you two, love, happiness, food!" With that they quitted the flat and Magnus led them to a small Greek restaurant that he knew. Irena suspected he took girlfriends here. The waiting staff seemed to know him well.

They dawdled over a delicious meal. Irena felt very relaxed and began to respond to their questions about life and home.

"In my country we were not the poorest – otherwise how could I have paid to come over here? From my job as a pharmacist assistant I saved and my parents helped me too – but things were getting worse. I worked for the state and sometimes they didn't pay us. Things were collapsing. After communism went everything was uncertain. Under communism you had a low wage but everything was cheap, many things were free.

Now you pay, pay for everything. I didn't want to wait until we joined the EU. I was getting older, I wanted a better life."

"But you ended up like a slave," said Colin. "Yes, like a slave." She raised her glass "to my friend Ilona." They saluted Ilona. "She is probably back in Romania by now." She thought of poor Ilona, how supportive she'd been, how they'd laughed together in hard times.

"To my beautiful fiancée," said Colin. Irena blushed. They drank several other toasts and wended their way back to the flat.

Magnus disappeared off to bed and Irena and Colin, once in their bedroom, dissolved into each other's arms.

The next day they did shop. She was utterly amazed at the shops, the quality, the variety. To Colin's delight Irena was thrifty, but she had good taste and picked out some items that suited her very well.

Exhausted by this outing, they found themselves in a coffee shop. "Remember this is how we met?" she said. How could he forget? How shy she seemed. He realised the shyness was fear, fear of Costa the gang boss, fear of being caught, being returned, in debt to the underworld bosses forever.

The girl in front of him was smiling, cheerful, lovable. He adored her. He would move heaven and earth to keep her – he would find a way.

They stayed three days at his parents. They obviously liked Irena and accepted the story that she was a student. Colin had never brought a girl home before, so they knew she was special.

She revelled in the scenery round Inverness but it made her homesick. She confessed this to Colin. "Well," he said "I've been thinking of ways to make you legal." "Truly?" she said eagerly.

"Well for one, you could hand yourself in – you'd be deported back to Romania, but while they process you here we'd be apart and we'd be apart while you're in Romania applying for re-entry.

Two – we cross back to the continent, travel across to the Hungary/Romania border and try to get back in."

"But I don't have my Romanian passport, Costa has it."

"Does he? Well the authorities may have it by now." That was worrying; did the UK authorities know she was here?

The team who had swooped on Costa and the work gang had arrested thirteen, the gang leader Costa, plus twelve others, eight men and four women. The lodgings had revealed the few pathetic belongings of the gang. There were more beds than the total thirteen but since there was always movement in these gangs this wasn't of special note.

The team had targets to meet. Illegals getting away was not what they wanted to hear at head office so they didn't hear about it.

Costa had many passports on him, more than 13 anyway – obviously he either had other illegals on his books or these were forgeries or stolen. So Irena's passport did not unduly attract suspicion. Nobody in the work gang gave any information nor of course did Costa. They were all too frightened of the underworld network and the consequences if they spoke.

Colin knew none if this. So he was working in the dark. They didn't want to be parted so option one seemed too hard.

Could he really get Irena and himself into continental Europe without needing passports? In theory you didn't need a passport to travel between EU countries but the UK airlines insisted on passports as a means of ID.

They would have to go overland.

The throbbing of the powerful diesels died away and the TDK workboat glided in to the pier. Steen Budrens stepped off followed by Colin and Irena – they all carried holdalls.

Steen was heading for his car and a drive to his home 2 kms away in the Dutch countryside.

So far Colin's plan had worked. TDK employed engineers from all over the UK but there were Dutch engineers on the Great Yarmouth windfarm project too. Holland had a lot of experience in wind turbine installation. The workboat regularly took the Dutch engineers home after a stint.

But Steen didn't drive straight home. He dropped Colin and Irena off at a motorway services on the Belgian autobahn from Zeebrugge.

Two hours later a container truck marked "ScotRom" pulled in. The driver met them in the coffee bar. Angus was 56, a retired welder. He worked for the ScotRom charity delivering clothes and second hand domestic appliances to Romania. He liked the driving and felt he was doing some good. Magnus had contacted him for Colin. "Remember the story is you're just hitch hikers I picked up" said Angus. "We'll be ok until the Hungary/Romania border, then you'll have to be creative."

For most of the journey they rode in the cab and ate with Angus. While he slept in the truck bunk behind the driver's seat, they slept amongst the bales of clothes. It was strange for Irena; like winding a film backward, only this time she could see the countryside – on the way over to the UK she had been hidden and the journey was experienced as a soundscape.

By the time they got to the Hungarian/Romanian border, Angus had become friends with them – he was sympathetic to their plight. He thought if they hid amongst the bales of cloth they would get through.

"They check lorries for people smuggling, and drugs going out, but not in."

Deep amongst the bales of cloth, Colin and Irena heard and felt the lorry slow at the checkpoint. They could hear a dog barking but it was farther away.

Through a tiny tear in the side tarpaulin Irena could see the outgoing trucks; moving down the trucks were border police with dogs – some were grouped round the first truck in the queue. People were being pulled from it. She shuddered. The awfulness of that journey across Europe came back; the cold, the fear of discovery. Yet here she was returning.

Their truck was waved through without a search. The ScotRom driver made regular trips to Romania; he even knew some of the guards.

As the vehicle picked up speed Irena felt so strange – back in her own country – legal.

They were married in the church of St Cyril in her home village. They had had to wait for four weeks for replacement papers to be produced, but now she had her ID card, a passport and marriage certificate.

Colin would have to return to work in a week's time. It would take time for Irena's application to join her husband to come through. They wanted to go together to the British Embassy to make the application.

One final thing he did before they went, was to settle her debt with the gang network.

Irena phoned the local contact and a meeting was arranged. Colin wanted proof that Irena was paying back the money she owed, but Davos, the local gang boss said, "we cannot give any paper, this would compromise us."

Colin insisted that they have proof, "your people have told me that Costa is still being held and that the British Authorities are questioning him and the other people caught with him."

Irena caught her breath. So Ilona was still being held too. "How will Costa or any other network member know Irena has paid her debt? Davos looked at Colin. "There is a way." He gestured to one of his henchmen. "This is Kala — he is one of my trustees. He owes me no debts, he has paid me back. He stays with me out of loyalty."

The gang boss lifted Kala's shirtsleeve — on the shoulder was a tattoo — a small tattoo of a green dragon.

Irena gasped. Colin looked incredulous.

"This tattoo is the sign that Kala has paid all his debts," said Davos looking at Irena.

Colin took Irena into a corner of the room.

"This is barbaric," he said

"But it is true" said Irena "I have heard it is how they do things. I want to do it. I want to be totally free of them." Colin looked at her. She was tough, much tougher inside than he had thought.

"OK" he said, turning back to Davos "but she is a girl — it has to go somewhere else less visible so she can wear a swimsuit or a bikini and, I must be present."

Davos grunted agreement.

In the salon Colin watched as the tattooist transferred the design onto Irena's midriff below the navel. The dragon looked small and benign in its green colouring. He watched as Irena winced while the needles did their work, his hand holding hers and feeling it clench his.

He could not believe they were here, doing this; that this was Europe in the 21st century — that this was how things were still done.

At last it was finished. Irena felt giddy as she got up. Davos said, "So, you have proof. All of us will know you have paid."

He picked up the bag of money and left.

Colin and Irena stepped out into the street. Her skin was still painful — "will be for a few days" said the tattooist.

When they went to the Embassy to apply for Irena's entry to the UK they found themselves struggling with a huge form. She hesitated over one question. It asked.. "any distinguishing marks?"

Still tender from the needles, Irena bent and wrote slowly but firmly — "dragon tattoo below the navel."

SARDINIA

The land was sparse, dry, scrub covered – the Maquis, juniper, myrtle, dwarf pine, wild rosemary. They were all more or less aromatic, the beating sun releasing a heady scent into the air. He walked down the track, his boots crunching on gravel. In the bay below, the sea, a bright Mediterranean blue lazily caressed the cliffs. He was searching for geckos – sunny days brought them out to bask. Cold rendered them inactive. He thought of his wife. She was like that. Back in Manchester she'd been a different person, morose, taciturn, cynical. Here she just flowered out. It was the sun. Briefly he pondered on a theory of weather as a treatment for mental states. The hyperactive should go to the cold places and those sluggish depressed souls to the sun. He could name it after himself, "McKinnon's Theory."

Every scientist secretly longed to have something named after them, a comet, an effect, a rule, a theory. A gecko darting round a boulder brought him back to the task in hand – he raised his camera. Back at the villa his wife Mary was putting the finishing touches to lunch – a simple Mediterranean one of Orecchietta with greens. She loved the little ears of Orecchietta pasta. She chopped the spring onions, garlic and chard and put them to sauté. Then she mixed them with the cooked pasta. She'd sprinkle the lot with gorgonzola, parmigiano, and peccorino.

"Beats Lancashire hotpot" she thought. "No, revise that" she said to herself – warming food for cold climates was right, even here it got cold in the winter, a bit of soup was welcome. But she didn't miss Manchester, the rain, the cloudiness, the crime, clubbing. When you were a student maybe – looking for excitement, searching for a mate but not now, she was happy here. This afternoon she was going to start on a new piece, well, not this afternoon, she meant this evening – there had to be siesta. It was impossible to think in the afternoon heat. The evening was warm but tolerable. Her work had changed, not only the vibrant earthy colours of her glazes but her pots and amphorae were more, well, fecund, rounded, pregnant, as if they were ready to split open like pea pods and explode seeds into the undergrowth.

Of course, *she* was pregnant – it was coming out in her work.

What was it, the heat or the light? She'd read that light quickens the growth of plants even more than the increasing warmth.

The light had struck in the eye like a physical blow when she had arrived in Sardinia. As an artist, but also just as a physical being, it seemed to penetrate her. She giggled, thinking of how the warmth had made her body come alive and respond to Scott's. Now they were more evenly matched in desire. Yes, this was the right move for them.

STEADY AND RELIABLE

The tunnel amplified the deep resonating sound of the boat's slow revving Perkins diesel engine. "Steady, reliable, steady, reliable, steady reliable" was what it said.

The roof was low and dripping – all these canal tunnels were like this. He was frightened of the dark as a child – even now, entering a long tunnel made him nervous, but the headlight on the prow of the boat gave him courage and the thought that the canal was only three feet deep at most, meant you could wade out if you broke down. Above the diesel he heard a softer fluid sound, water from the bow wave rippling along the walls, slipping into the gloom astern.

Strange thoughts went through your head in a tunnel. Once he had imagined he was a spermatozoa heading for the womb – poor little buggers, at least he had the light and a mug of tea. He always made himself one before entering – it sort of steadied him and helped him concentrate.

In the past, the cabin lights would have blazed as his wife pottered inside the narrowboat. Not now – this time he was on his own.

"Don't get morbid," he told himself. "You've got to realise" his uncle had once said "that basically you're on your own in life." Uncle Harry was a dour Yorkshireman, as dour as you can get.

Fred didn't feel like uncle Harry. Fred always felt connected to everything. To his engines for a start. An engine was like a living thing – it responded to care and gave you back good service in return. The boat itself, snug and cosy, was a little cocoon on a journey like this. The open canal was alive with birds, fish, people – you were never "alone." You could feel separate sometimes but other times you felt just part of it all.

His wife hadn't been able to relate to the boat or the wildlife. She needed people close around her. He needed people too but not to feel he existed. He didn't feel lonely here on the canal. She did. She seemed to want more interaction with him than he could give. When the children had grown up she became restless, moody, depressed even, as if her purpose had gone. He wasn't enough for her. He was also, he felt, too familiar, a beaten path on which she knew every twist and turn, or thought she did.

The boat's note changed slightly as the current quickened. His wife wasn't a slow revver like the Perkins, he mused – more of an outboard. That's what had attracted him to her years ago. Maybe his slower, reliable beat had suited her then – stabilised her.

Thoughts of stabilisation made him recall that he must pump out the forward bilge compartment.

A tiny dot of light grew into an ever expanding half circle as the tunnel end approached. His tension eased – soon he would be out in the sunlight.

He hadn't expected her to leave, but that she had gone off with that plumber, that's what really shook him. She had even said to him "I'm fed up with steady and reliable, if I want steady and reliable I can buy a Volvo."

She said she had cooked and cleaned for years now, she wanted escape, excitement, travel, variety. He was silent. He too had sacrificed, kept a steady job he didn't particularly like, to keep the family.

The shock of her leaving had made him re-examine himself – "was reliable, predictable, such a bad thing?" For his kids he always felt they needed that stability, to know where they were, supported, that their parents were there. That's what gutted him most now – the nest not only empty, but destroyed. The children, though young adults, had been able to return home to familiar territory if things got tough out there.

Everything was changed. Now they had to decide to see him or her, or visit both in turn. They couldn't go "home" because the house had been sold, the assets divided, the love divided.

He tied up next to 'The Yellow Parrot', the first pub after the tunnel. Most canal boaters had a drink there after the tunnel, some to steady their nerves, others to celebrate coming into the light, the rebirthing.

He had just settled himself outside at a table when his mobile rang. Jenny his daughter wanted to bring a friend on the boat at the weekend.

Jenny had been angry at her mum for leaving her dad and at the way her mum had done it – i.e. with the plumber. Jenny thought the whole thing "tacky" and seemed to feel mum should have got past sexual feelings at her age. It was a new thing to have to grapple with your parents' sexuality – not something you normally wanted to face. Not only that, now they were split they were more explicitly individual, not collectively "your parents." She gravitated to her dad because he seemed to be just as he had always been. Mum seemed to have transformed herself into a totally different being. She had changed her hair of course and her clothes. Jenny hadn't said this to her but she felt her mum had gone "tarty" – bleached blonde, frilly dresses, high heels.

Jenny had felt the loss of the family home acutely. All those past certainties, her room, the familiar toys, the wallpaper, the family gatherings with cousins – now all only photos, memories.

When she had driven past the house recently to visit a friend she felt such pangs of loss that she stopped the car farther on and just cried.

She was, after all, only eighteen. She hadn't established her own home yet; she didn't even have a steady boyfriend. She felt as if everything around her was jelly, unreliable.

Fred was aware of some of this. He sensed his daughter's confusion and anger. He felt helpless really but realised that if he was there for her, supportive, it would help.

He had readily agreed to her coming – he wanted to see her, and her friend, they would liven the boat up. He finished his pint and returned on board. They'd be here tomorrow, he had better spruce up the cabins.

She could easily accommodate six, eight at a push. After all she was 60 feet long and well equipped. Two double bed cabins and two singles.

When his son had come to stay with his wife they had fitted in fine. He liked his son's wife, Minda. He recalled how caring she'd been. She was Malayan, a nurse, practical, firm but sensitive.

Hugo, Fred's son was 23 now. He had taken the break up less badly but still felt confused. Having his own family unit helped, but he felt torn between his mum and dad. He had been the apple of his mum's eye – now she was preoccupied with the plumber. "Was he jealous? Surely not," he told himself, "but yes," he resented her affections being diverted from himself – even though he loved his wife, he still craved attention from his mother.

And so Hugo visited his dad with Minda, while if Hugo saw his mum at all, it was when she came on her own to visit him. It was easier without the plumber around.

All of the family relationships had been altered, shifted, remade. Some had become more fleeting, uncertain.

"Christmasses and birthdays are going to be hellish" thought Fred. Those family gatherings you took for granted, how would they work? Everyone delicately treading around each other's feelings.

As he tidied the galley he could see through the kitchen porthole another narrow boat chugging past, the deep beat of its diesel echoing "steady, reliable, steady, reliable."

THE CHARITY TURKEY

Karen Denman was standing by the front door of the house discreetly smoking a cigarette. She didn't want to smoke in front of the kids, it was bad for them and she wouldn't want them to take it up, but, just now, she needed it.

Rab had left two weeks ago, came back for his stuff, said he was off, had enough. A woman at the co-op had told her he'd gone off with a lass just out of school.

It had not been great, their marriage, but it worked after a fashion. He'd cooled a lot since the kids came along – he seemed irritated as they got older, maybe he couldn't stand the competition for her attention.

The kids, Harry four and Sheena eight, were devastated. They didn't understand – they thought it was their fault.

For herself, she felt abused, gutted, sick to her stomach, already dumped for a younger model. God, she was only 32! She was left with all the problems too, the debts, the council tax, the rent.

She'd been to the social and it was in hand, but, for now, it was a mess. It wouldn't be sorted 'til after Xmas.

Xmas – it was December the 20th, what a time to leave, the bastard.

Well she'd do her best – she started to think of what she could do to make it something for the kids.

Just then a small red 3 wheeler pulled up outside her gate. A man and woman in uniform got out. The bloody cops – what next, what has he done now?

They came up the path like no police she knew, beaming from ear to ear.

Then she twigged, Sally Ann, hoping for a donation no doubt – well, they could think again.

She stubbed out her fag as they drew level. "Mrs Denman?" said the woman. "Yes" said Karen. "We've heard about your misfortune, we'd like you to accept this." The man held out a large box. "We get donations from people, anonymously, at this time of the year and we like to distribute them where they're needed."

Seeing the worried look on Karen's face he continued. "Its a turkey, a big one. The lady who handed it in said not to stuff it – it's well stuffed already." He omitted to add that she had winked at him as she handed it over. He thought at the time she was giving him the eye and was flattered.

Karen hesitated, then took the box, "thank you" she said.

They turned and walked off – more people to visit no doubt. She was in no position, she knew, to afford a turkey. The problem had been preying on her mind. Her heavy heart lifted a little. She turned back into the house – she placed the box in the kitchen and went in to give her kids a cuddle and plan the decorations.

The house depressed her, she thought, as she and her daughter pinned up spirals of crepe paper. It was a downbeat council estate in need of an upgrade. Their house had been due for new sinks and windows for some time and there were damp patches on the ceilings. Fat chance of her being able to do much herself now that Rab had scarpered.

Her own family had been good – presents for the kids. Just as well, she couldn't afford anything you'd call a big present. Harry wouldn't notice but Sheena was at that age where she was only too conscious of what her friends had – it wasn't that Sheena was too materialistic, it was just that they, all the girls of her age, were.

Karen's mum often went on about how spoiled kids were today compared to her childhood – it didn't help. "Its different now" she reminded her mum.

On Xmas day, Karen made an extra effort. She took the turkey out of the fridge and read the label for the defrosting and the cooking time and got the bird in the oven by ten o'clock.

She and Sheena prepared the veg – the trimmings were very important, they made it really – brussels, bread sauce, apple sauce cranberry sauce and gravy. Luckily, Harry always had a sleep for a couple of hours about eleven.

By 12 o'clock things were looking good. She and Sheena were in the living room laying the table. Harry was on the couch with his little blue bunny blanket over him. The TV was on, Sheena wanted to watch a film.

Suddenly there was a large bang and a tongue of blue flame shot out of the kitchen door followed by the sound of cracking and burning, smoke billowed out into the room.

For seconds Karen, stunned, stared in disbelief, then she looked for her children. Sheena had been thrown to the floor with a cut above her eye. She wasn't moving. Harry had been shielded by the back of the couch. He was awake now and crying. Karen bent over Sheena. She opened her eyes and looked at her mum. She seemed dazed and confused. Karen's next thought was to get them out of the house as soon as possible. She yanked Sheena to her feet and grabbed Harry in his blanket and made for the front door. Behind her the fire had got hold and smoke and flames billowed out after her.

Outside, neighbours began to gather, someone had called the Fire Brigade. The upstairs had caught now and the smoke, brown, black, dense was streaming out of the windows. She watched in horror.

The fire engine arrived. A senior fireman, directed to her by neighbours, checked if everyone was out.

Then firemen were all around her, directing hoses at the windows, door and roof.

One of the firemen led her back from the flames to the fire engine.

Her senses were heightened now, she was incredibly alert, aware.

She saw in front of her a face, framed in a yellow helmet, a handsome face, rugged, practical; he was asking her something. He wanted to know her name and address and details of the kids, was there a husband? She must have given the answers, because he stopped for a moment. He asked if there was someone she could go to stay with; it was then she burst out crying. She was crying with anger, she was bloody homeless, manless. When Rab had gone she'd at least got the house – now it was burnt to a crisp. Did she say all this through her tears? Later she couldn't remember.

Andrew, the fire officer in question, listened attentively – people in shock often said the wildest things. The woman in front of him clutching one child to her breast and another to her side was a slim attractive blond with blue green eyes. The absent husband had been mad to leave her.

Andrew was being as professional as he could – he'd been given this part of the job because he was "empathetic", his boss had told him.

He put his arm on her shoulder and said supportive things to her.

When she looked up at him they held each others gaze for more than a moment.

She opted to stay with her mother in her cramped flat.

The policewoman who drove her there, said social services had been contacted and a few days later they called about a new apartment that was available – "Would she like to view it?" Leaving Harry with mum, she and Sheena looked it over. Newly built, clean, a modern kitchen, bedrooms, one for each of them – lovely, she said "yes, yes." They even supplied what they called temporary furniture – to her it seemed great. Moving in the next week took all of ten minutes.

The very next day after moving, a heavy knock at the door revealed Andrew – the fireman. "Remember me?" he said with a smile "How could I ever forget?" she said. "I've come to give you the forensic report – about what started the fire." "Oh" she said, a little disappointed.

"There was a bottle of whisky stuffed inside that turkey. When it got to a certain temperature it just exploded." continued Andrew. Karen couldn't help laughing.

Andrew smiled but was confused. She told him about the Sally Ann turkey, then she told him how things had been that Xmas day. Indeed she talked and talked, he was, after all, empathetic. He watched her closely as she talked. Then she said "what did I say to you on the day of the fire?" "Em, a lot of things, you were angry, it's quite common you know" he continued – he looked into her blue green eyes and was aware of that feeling he'd had on the day she was rescued.

He got up, said he had to go but as he opened the door he said "would you like to come out for a pub lunch?" he saw her expression, "yes I meant all of you – on Sunday?" She was silent for a second then said "Yes, yes I would."

FOUND

Karen kept her head down against the rain as it beat down. She was cycling home from Alness and her job at the video shop. Dull, dreary, depressing work but all she could find for her year out before Uni.

As she rounded the bend on the little highland road she suddenly saw the boot of a car, a blue BMW, sticking up at an odd angle half hanging over the ravine on the left of the road. Glass was spattered around, dark tyre marks burnt on the road. Most of the car was pushed deep into the bushes at the top of the ravine.

She stopped and dismounted. She crept closer, the car suddenly slipped downwards – she jumped, then to her horror it slid slowly down, gathering speed until she heard an enormous thump and then a "whump" as an explosion burst upwards. Stunned, she watched the bright orange flames burn with ferocity. She felt shock and horror. How long she stood there she did not know. She found herself looking around in the verge into the bushes. Perhaps the driver had crawled out. Amongst the torn and mangled brambles and willows she found a black briefcase, a businessman's case, quite fat looking, leather covered with brass handles.

She picked it up, and still dazed, mounting her bike she cycled home carefully. She met no cars on the road – she seldom did. Her home was a small croft house set back from this minor road.

She cycled up the lane, automatically putting her bike in the woodshed as usual. She left the briefcase there too.

She stumbled into the house. Mum and Dad were not home – they had gone to Auntie Jean's – they wouldn't be in 'til 8.00 p.m. She picked up the phone and dialled 999. She reported the accident – "No", she did not get the number. "Yes, blue BMW." "No", she did not, could not see anybody in it.

An hour later her parents found her sitting at the kitchen table. She gabbed out the story about the car, the police – her mother could see she was in shock.

The police arrived at 10 o'clock. She was tired now. They quizzed her about the car, but she had little to add.

That night, exhausted, she fell into a deep sleep only to wake with a dream of the car exploding.

The next day was Sunday. She got up late. There was never anything to do in this out of the way place anyway. Karen was desperate to get away. Her foster parents were okay but they smothered her somehow. Everything was boring here – except for the car crash. My God _that_ was awesome!

Then she remembered the briefcase – why had she taken it? Why not? She had got into trouble before for taking stuff. Anyway, no-one's asked for it. The driver probably won't need it where he is. She felt bad in thinking of him, but it was true.

She got out of bed, got dressed and went out to the woodshed. There it was, tucked in behind a woodpile near the bike. Nice bag, worth a bit – what was in it?

It was heavy. Taking it on her knee she flicked open the catches – she gasped – neatly stacked piles of £20 notes filling the briefcase met her gaze. She shut it again and looked around.

The woodshed door was out of sight of the house, but Karen was a past master at concealment. No-one was in the door frame – she opened it again, yes it was true. She closed it quickly and placed it further back.

The police might be looking for it. She'd wait. Over a week went past. Then the paper reported that the car belonged to a drug dealer from Glasgow, but no foul play was suspected. What little remained of his body revealed a high drug content in the tissue. He'd overdosed then crashed and was burnt in the fire.

Karen realised that if anyone suspected or knew there was money they would assume it had burned in the fire – so no-one was looking for the money. Still she had better take no action for a while. She hadn't counted it, but it looked like thousands. She itched to spend it, but she knew she would come under suspicion if she started spending.

It had happened before – the time she nicked £20 from the children's home – various shops in the village had told the houseparent she was spending freely – she was grounded for ages.

No, she would have to think this out. She was used to going into a shell, cutting off. She'd learned that in care, not to give, in fear of losing something yet again. She'd never known her father – her mother had died – "in childbirth," the houseparent had said, and later her elderly grandmother hadn't been able to cope. When she had died there was no-one left but the children's home. Then she'd been fostered, but she wasn't open, ready to be loved. The bit of her that could have responded was deeply hidden – she protected it from hurt. Hiding the money was like that; it was easy to shut out its existence.

She kept working at the video shop. Cycling home was difficult – each time she had to pass the tyre marks and the gash in the bushes and each time she thought of the explosion.

Her foster parents found her morose, uncommunicative – well, more than usual, anyway. They put it down to the after effects of the crash.

One day, while the video shop was quiet, a young policeman came in. He was looking for a video, 'Gladiator' – she helped him find it on the shelves – she knew them inside out now. He said, "Aren't you the girl from the crash?" "I interviewed you that night."

She genuinely couldn't recognise his face.

"It's alright, you were in shock. I recognised that straight away – people often don't remember things."

She asked innocently about drug dealers. He told her how it was getting harder for them these days. He explained how banks were alerted to look out for people depositing large cash sums and how banks made it harder for people to open new accounts without clear IDs. "No," he wasn't in the drug squad; he was on traffic, he said. He paid for his video and left.

Karen realised that to get any serious benefit from this money was not going to be easy. Sure, she could spend a little here and there, but £200,000! Big chunks spent would show up.

It was a month after the crash and she was in the video shop idly reading a women's magazine. "Trace your ancestors – full service, find out where you came from." For Karen this struck a chord. She desperately needed to find out about her father and her mother, she didn't know who she was. £200 it said. That shouldn't arouse any suspicion. The address was an office in Inverness.

That Saturday she told her foster mum she was going into Inverness to do a little shopping. She took the bus in from the road end. It took an hour as it stopped and started for the passengers. In Inverness she quickly found the office – one floor up. "Ancestor Search" it said on the glass door. Pushing in she found a youngish woman at a computer. The room was pleasant and smelt of beeswax. Books lined shelves behind her.

The young woman introduced herself. "I'm Fiona Matheson," she said, "How can I help?"

Karen explained what she wanted. Miss Matheson's response was businesslike. "Tracing your mother's family will probably be easy – your father – well, that will involve getting in touch with Social Work, but you have the right now to find out." Karen's heart sank, Social Work, would she *ever* be shot of them – but the drive to find out was strong and overcame any negative feeling she had.

Miss Matheson said she needed the £200 now because some of the searches cost money and there were expenses such as telephone and photocopying. Karen handed over the notes. Miss Matheson made no comment at notes rather than a cheque and popped the money into a drawer.

"How long will it take?"

"It varies," said Miss Matheson, "Sometimes weeks, sometimes months. Ring me at the end of next week to check on progress."

Karen left and headed for a nearby coffee bar – the tension that had built up because of the money, because she was tackling something big in her life, had drained away gradually in Miss Matheson's office – she had seemed so professional, didn't ask nosy questions about her or her money. Sure, she needed her name, date of birth, what she knew of her mother and other details like that, but no questions loaded with emotion, just factual.

She felt a sense of power, something was happening and she had initiated it. She felt a little high.

Miss Matheson was good. By the end of week one she'd mapped out her mother's family tree; MacAskills, from Skye originally, with MacDonalds, and MacLeans marrying in – crofters/fishermen and, like many highland families, they had drifted to the town – in this case Inverness. Her grandfather had been a joiner and her grandmother a cook. She hadn't known that.

Her father's side had taken longer – loads of faffing about with Social Work. Three weeks later Miss Matheson called her at the video shop and asked her to come in next Saturday. In her office Miss Matheson explained the trouble she'd had getting the information.

"It appears your father was not Scottish." she said tantalisingly.

"He was Spanish. His name was Enrico Chavez. He was a merchant seaman on a small cargo ship that for a time called in regularly to Inverness."

Karen sat quietly, stunned but excited.

"I've only got as far as identifying the shipping line he worked for – to go further will cost more."

Karen nodded. Of course she would pay more "Another £200?"

"Yes." said Miss Matheson. Karen had anticipated this and had brought the money with her.

Again Miss Matheson popped the notes into the desk drawer. She handed Karen copies of the information she had researched to date. It included a birth certificate. "I'll phone you at work when I find out more."

Karen was slotting videos away in the shop two weeks later when the phone rang. Miss Matheson had tracked down her father to an address in Santa Cruz, a fishing port on the Costa Blanca – he still worked for the same shipping company.

In Miss Matheson's office the following Saturday, Miss Matheson warned her not to get her hopes too high. "He may not want to know you. He could be a drunk, a wife beater, you don't know, so don't be too starry eyed – I've seen this go wrong before" she said. She gave Karen the details.

There was no question. She was going to Spain to find this father of hers. Flights were so cheap now that it was within the bounds of financial possibility that she had saved enough, so when she told her foster parents she planned to go on holiday with a friend to Spain they saw it in a positive light – lots of young people did it – but just who was she going to go with? Then she had an idea.

The next Saturday she visited Miss Matheson and put it to her. Would she come with her? Karen explained that she trusted her and valued her experience. She also explained that she would pay for the fares and expenses. That swung it. Rarely had Miss Matheson been able to follow through an enquiry to this point – and never abroad. She would, she argued to herself, be able to give Karen the support she needed.

By the time they got to Santa Cruz they were both exhausted with the travelling and the excitement of what they were undertaking. The port was a busy commercial one – huge container ships and tankers were tied up at massive jetties – cranes, trucks and forklifts busied to and fro.

Karen was suddenly hit with the knowledge that this was her father's work – these ships and docks. He had been a fantasy, then a little bit of veil had been lifted, now some of his reality was here.

In the hotel overlooking the bay, Miss Matheson quickly found out where the shipping offices were, from the barman, who spoke English well. She told him they were relatives of Enrico Chavez and that they wanted to meet him.

The barman laughed. "He always has luck with the ladies!" he explained "Look — sure I know him — I will ring him now to meet you, say, for 7 o'clock, okay?" After the call the barman told them a little about Enrico. He was about forty. He was ashore now, a manager in the shipping line, he'd been at sea for about twenty years — got up to Captain. Was he well off? Well, yes and no — he had a big pay, but he spent it all on his boat. "You can see it out in the bay." A large white motor yacht lay anchored there. "The Hidalgo — she's a beauty."

"Is he married?" said Miss Matheson suddenly, a professional question, no doubt.

"Well", said the barman, "he was, but it broke up. He was away at sea too much."

"Children?" persisted Miss Matheson.

"No. He regrets that very much." replied the barman. "It has made him a little, how you say, morose."

As the clock approached 7.00 p.m. they sat in the hotel lobby trying not to look anxious or curious. At each entrance they both swivelled their heads to the door.

A dark haired, well-dressed, bearded man of medium build approached them from within the hotel. "Ladies, you are expecting me?"

Karen found her lips dry, words wouldn't come out. Miss Matheson took over. She invited him to join them for dinner and he accepted.

It was there that Miss Matheson explained why they had come to see him. Bewilderment, then astonishment, then disbelief — "Are you sure?" – then reassured, joy swept over his face. He took Karen's hands in his. "A daughter!" he exclaimed. There were many questions from Karen and from Enrico.

Enrico insisted they come out that night to see his yacht. It was certainly grand and spotless, with spacious cabins, ensuite showers and a jacuzzi. Karen could see it was his pride and joy.

"But", said Enrico, he was thinking of selling. "It has been very expensive getting it to this standard and I owe the bank a lot. My idea was to take people on paid trips up the coast, catering for them – a sort of luxury holiday."

Karen's mind had been on a roller coaster all day, but with clarity she saw how she could help her father.

He insisted they stay on the boat for the week they had planned. As the days went by she realised she loved the sea, the boat. Did her father care for her? She was sure of it. He was interested in everything about her, her past, her present. He confessed to her his love of the boat was great – so great it had wrecked his marriage – he'd learnt from that. He told them that while the boat was important, it was not everything. He asked her to come and live with him on the boat – she was overcome. Somehow the boat seemed secure, protective.

She asked to see him alone on deck. Miss Matheson said she understood and stayed below watching television.

Karen explained that she had money – quite a lot of money – nobody knew about it except her. She wanted him to have it to pay off the boat, but she said they would become partners – legal partners. Karen said he'd have to understand that trust was difficult for her as she'd always had to look after herself – he was not to be insulted. He looked at his daughter – he understood – it's what he would have proposed anyway – even families can fall out.

Sometime after Karen and Miss Matheson got back, a sleek motor yacht moored in Inverness Harbour. With Miss Matheson's help, Karen had explained to her foster parents the ancestral research that had led to the discovery of Karen's real father. Karen's decision to go and live with her father was discussed at length, but eventually accepted. She was eighteen, she could do as she wanted. They were somewhat relieved – she'd not been an easy girl – it was like sitting on a volcano – not quite knowing when it might explode.

Karen insisted on carrying her own bags on board and stowing them below. As the boat pulled out she waved goodbye to Miss Matheson and her foster parents. When they were well out to sea she went below, opened the holdall that held the money, and looked at it for a moment. She zipped the bag shut and then went on deck. She edged close to her father at the wheel as he began explaining how to steer the ship.

HIDDEN MOSQUE

In a far off land beyond the mountain lay a desert country. To some it was bleak and treeless, to others it was magical. At night the stars sprinkled the sky as if on a dark blue carpet. In the day time, the sun beat down on a magnificent landscape of rocks and sand, sand that sometimes rolled in huge dunes towards the horizon. If you were a crow you would look down and see here and there a little patch of green – an oasis where date palms surrounded a well.

Hasan was 10. Because he was a boy he could roam where he wanted but he didn't go far into the desert. It was easy to get lost and you could die from the heat of the blazing sun. There were bandits in the desert too – they could rob you or worse, kill you, or sell you into slavery.

But his father often went with the camel caravan to the city of Tirgiz to buy salt, metal goods and coffee. It was safer in the caravan with all the others and the men carried rifles.

His father would tell him stories of the trips and of exciting happenings. Often the caravan travelled at night to avoid the bandits and because it was cooler.

On one trip they met a wandering holy man or imam as they are called in that country. They offered him coffee and a share of their meal as was the custom. The holy man blessed them and then a curious thing happened. He said he carried an important secret and that, as he was old, he felt it was right to pass it on to another, younger man. He would select from the caravan the man most worthy to keep the secret, and the way he did this was like this.

Each member of the caravan had to say what he wished for most. Some said gold, some said silver or gems – some wanted camels. "What did you say father?" said Hasan. "To get home safely", said Hasan's father.

The holy man then seemed to tell several men the secret. When he came to Hasan's father he said "Because you wish for no goods or camels you cannot be bought. I have told the others nothing of value, but to you I will tell the real secret."

"There is a hidden place, a beautiful mosque," said the holy man "that all men could see and enter if they had the right keys."

"Is it far?" said my father. "It is far for some, close for others," said the holy man.

"The first key you have – it is lack of greed. The second key is to care for all living creatures even your enemies. The third key is to be truthful in word and deed. The fourth key is to show no anger or hate. The fifth key is to take only what is freely given. – when you have all these keys you can open the door and enter." "And what is in this mosque?" said Hasan. His father told him that the holy man had said that in the mosque was the greatest wealth that a man can have – a constant sense of joy.

Hasan wondered at these words – yes, joy was a good thing to have. With it you would not need gold or silver or camels.

When he felt joy he seemed to float like the air in the heat of the day, shimmering above the sand.

The Choosing is the emptying of the heart of the all things other than the search for completion. This takes the form of a visualisation that the body is empty, and that all thoughts have left it for a moment, during which time true thoughts flood in.

Hujwiri, a Sufi sage.

ISTIFA

(The Choosing)

As she lay by the side of the road she could taste the sand in her mouth yet she was aware of the faint perfume of a flowering bush somewhere out there in the desert – cars continued to whoosh by so close to her body that she could feel the hot dry wind as they passed. She wanted, needed to move away from their path. It was one of them that had struck her – hitting her backpack spinning her round and down by the side of the main road to El Kebir. She felt angry at the car, at herself – some of her friends had been right – this was a dangerous thing to do, hitch hike in this country – a girl dressed in European clothes commanded no respect when alone. Had they aimed the car at her? She saw clearly in her mind the youths in the white Mercedes.

She heard a car stop, the doors slam and feet stepping quickly towards her – voices in Arabic, a face leaning over her, a young face, then another – she could not find words.

They lifted the pack gently off her and then hands bore her into a car – she remembered later the red seats and the smell of leather – she felt herself drifting off, off into a deep blackness.

She awoke to the sounds of birds chirping. She saw a ceiling above her of latticed palm fronds dappled with yellow shafts from a pierced screen window. Someone moved next to her bed – a woman dressed in a blue gandora spoke to her in Arabic – the tone suggesting she was relieved to see her awake.

A young man knocked and entered – in halting English he introduced himself as Hasan. He asked her forgiveness – when she asked "For what?" he explained he was driving the car that had hit her. An oncoming car was approaching him so close he had to pull over to his side of the road, too late, he'd seen her and clipped her backpack. He had turned round and come back as soon as he could. This was his mother's house. A doctor was coming soon.

Studying Hasan's open countenance Helena was aware of his gentle brown eyes, his strong beard darkened jaw line and his full dark hair – a small shiver of excitement ran through her body but then he was gone. Hasan had said something about a doctor.

Did she need a doctor? She felt her bandaged head – tried to move her legs – they seemed okay – mostly she seemed tired, weak, helpless – too helpless to protest, to demand, to insist as she usually might have done.

This was obviously the house of people who were poor she thought. The walls were bare red mud – apart from the bed there was no furniture – it seemed clean. As she was thinking this, another person entered in a black jellaba – the outer garment worn by Muslim women in this country.

Removing the jellaba revealed a woman in green top and slacks. "I am Samira Bin Hassi, the doctor," she said.

Helena must have reacted because the woman said, "Yes, we do have women doctors!" Dr Bin Hassi careful checked her over, announcing at the end of the examination "You may have concussion – Hasan's people will send for me if you develop certain symptoms in the next twenty-four hours – I will also call on you during that period." Helena offered to pay the doctor, but she said Hasan had already arranged her fee.

The doctor left. Hasan's mother, Ama, gave Helena a drink of cold milk — Helena drifted off into sleep. She dreamt she was at home — she was in bed in the big family house in Scotland. Her parents weren't there. She was being looked after by Bessie the housekeeper, tucked in and fed porridge laced with honey. She woke with a start. Where were her parents? She remembered, yes, father at that time was in London at his business, mother had gone to New York with a friend to a fashion show. Helena often found herself alone at Kindrummy House in the summer — alone, that is, apart from the servants.

She was twenty when her parents died during a private jet flight to the Bahamas. Helena then found herself truly alone, alone but wealthy. How wealthy she'd never imagined until the will set out the various shares, bonds and properties. She had friends, of course, and their numbers seemed to increase after the will became common knowledge amongst her set.

Six empty, hollow, months after the death of her parents, she'd decided to start this trip alone; a hitch hiking holiday through Morocco. Why? Why indeed? — her friends were appalled — they reeled off reasons why not — flies, heat, danger of attack. She'd persisted in her plans. All her life she'd been in a channel, a cosy wealthy channel that had led her from kindergarten to private school — to art school — she felt she'd never had to struggle She became aware that she moved within a limited group of friends, a certain protected strata of society. She'd wanted to jerk herself out of that, to somewhere that no one knew of her wealth. Once people knew you were worth millions of pounds the game was lost — they fawned, they begged, they pursued. Even if you could avoid the "hingers on", as Bessie called them, there was always loads of paperwork, signing that had to be done. Her wealth was a live thing that had to be managed, exercised like a racehorse.

By the third day she was able to get up — she'd survived the crucial period when concussion might have shown itself. The doctor recommended rest for a few weeks.

She discovered the house had a flat roof. She sat there in the day on a beautiful carpet chatting to the doctor who, because she spoke

English, had become Helena's source of information and a sounding board.

Hasan, it turned out, was a carpet dealer. The doctor explained about the special place of carpets in the Middle East both as art objects, but also as having a religious and mystical aspect. The carpet's design represented a garden, suggesting the garden that was promised by Allah to all believers in paradise. Indeed the word paradise was an Arabic word meaning garden. Now Helena fully understood the origin of the stories she'd been told in the west about "magic" carpets.

Hasan had made it clear she could stay as long as she wanted. "Our house is your house," he had said. She felt calm here, free within the house.

As well as the roof there was a tiled courtyard where the children played – not Hasan's children but his brother's. There were two families here, Hasan and his mother, Yosef his brother, Yosef's wife Malika and their three children, Jabril, Khazed and Mohammed.

The house was bigger than she had first thought. All rooms looked out on or opened out onto the courtyard. On the ground floor were bedrooms for the family and a reception room called a majles. On the first floor were family rooms – large open rooms, called moakar, with carpets, cushions and soft low seats called diwan. The roof was used for sleeping during the summer, but also for sitting out and chatting. Ama kept doves up there in a little dovecote. Also, there were pots with herbs grown for cooking and, of course, it was here the washing was spread out to dry on wash days. The women could look down from the roof onto the street to see what was going on and often called to other women on nearby roofs. There was a lot of joking and gossiping and general fun as they went about their tasks.

As soon as the men left for work there was almost a party atmosphere – the house rang with the children's voices as they played games throughout it. Someone tuned in a radio to Arab dance music on Radio Moroc.

With two servants to help with the heavier things the housework did not take the women long and they stopped for long chats about everything and to play with the children.

Helena had never done any housework – but somehow she now enjoyed it. Her few words of Arabic increased till after a month she could follow what was going on in a rudimentary way.

She learnt of the "hudud" – the sacred frontiers, the rules governing behaviour, although the women seemed to break 'the rules' fairly frequently.

One day she found herself thinking that although the women were confined in many ways to the house and to certain trips outside there were at least boundaries, whereas in western life she had none. With unlimited resources she was free to travel, but in the life of the inner being she was empty – she had no husband, no children, no place that was home and few friends she could trust.

She discussed these things gradually and more openly with the doctor, Samira. As a doctor, Samira was freer – because of her profession she could enter houses, she had male and female colleagues and moved freely in the hospital. True, she wore the jellaba and veil in the street, but she laughed and said it allowed you to look at the men without them knowing.

The doctor's comment about men made her think of Hasan – he had touched something in her, and he was very handsome and kind. Her heart leapt when she thought of him. She had wanted to see more of him, but she knew it was not the Muslim custom for men and women to be alone unless married. She asked Samira had she a boyfriend? "Yes," said Samira, a colleague, a paediatrician, who had won her heart as she watched him gently tending to the preemies, the premature babies in the hospital.

"Will you marry?" said Helena. Samira said "It's going that way, I am going to tell his sister to tell him to hurry up and ask me."

"Is that how you do it here?" asked Helena "get a relative to prompt the man?"

"Not always," said Samira. "Some marriages are still arranged, but today girls want to marry for love – so we help the process along ourselves."

Dr Bin Hassi was no fool – working with patients each day often led you to be able to read their thoughts. She sensed that Helena was drawn to Hasan. "Of course, Hasan has no sister, but I am his cousin," said Samira. That, thought Helena, explains a lot – how Samira seemed to be at ease in Hasan's home – more than if she had been a stranger. "Hasan needs to marry," continued Samira "he would make a good father."

"What are the attitudes here to marrying foreigners though?" said Helena.

"If you are an unbeliever it would not go well, but if you became a Muslim then you would find acceptance almost total."

"What does that entail, becoming a Muslim?" asked Helena.

"So you *are* interested!", exclaimed Samira. "I told Hasan so."

Helena blushed – then they both laughed. "I will come tomorrow and explain what it entails," said Samira.

That night Helena couldn't sleep. Was this the step she should take? What were the dangers? She had never been close to her father, but he had once talked to her about business. "Always examine the downside risk." She thought of what could go wrong – was there a "get out" clause? She had heard that divorce for Muslim women was easy, too easy for the men! She didn't want to be trapped in a marriage that went bad or snarled up in difficult Muslim laws.

The way Samira explained it, becoming a Muslim seemed very simple. You had to state before the Mullah that you believed in God and that Mohamed was his prophet. Men were expected to pray five times a day but women were excused this as they went to the mosque infrequently. You have to give alms to the poor and if possible go on pilgrimage to Mecca. You should also spread the faith. This was called "jihad". The wedding ceremony was quite different from that in the west. A marriage contract (the nikah) was arranged and recorded with the Qu'adi, the judge, and witnessed by two competent adults. Under the contract the dowry, the mahr, paid by the husband to the wife, was specified. This is her money to give her financial security and she can use it as she sees fit. Islamic women do not take their husband's name but keep their own identity to emphasise the status of family, and lineage. The Koran says a Muslim woman, single or married, is an individual in her own right with the right to own and dispose of her property and earnings.

There was no religious ceremony in the mosque to resemble our church service. A big party took place with separate celebrations for the men and for the women. The men often congregated in the courtyard of the house with music and food. The women often had their party on the first floor behind the pierced screens so they could see the men. At some point the bride brought the bridegroom into the women's party to show him off.

Helena asked Samira bluntly "What is the downside risk?" and when Samira looked blank at this phrase Helena said "What are the bad points?"

"Well, said Samira, "If you change your mind, i.e. don't want to be Muslim after becoming one then that is called "apostasy" and that is punishable by death."

"What?" said Helena aghast.

"Also, if you are in a country which is governed by Sharia law you can be stoned for adultery and have an extremity removed for theft, you know, like a hand or foot. There are also rules governing the separation of the sexes in public places and women should cover up when in the street – arms, legs and the hijab, the veil, but not all countries are so strict and only a few Muslim countries have the Sharia law – it doesn't apply in Morocco. In some countries, like Turkey, women wear western dress all the time."

Looking at Helena, who seemed downcast, Samira added, "There is one other thing – the Koran says a man can have four wives!"

"Four?" said Helena in amazement.

"But," said Samira, "not many do now. It's too expensive!" and laughed. "Anyway, Morocco is passing a new law to restrict new marriages to one."

Samira left for a doctors' conference, leaving Helena in a state of confusion. This was a big step. From her present understanding, accepting all that Islam presented, meant considerable risks and pitfalls. Yet she was drawn to the life and atmosphere it created, one of order, strict boundaries, containment – that led to a sense of security, knowing where you are. Did she have strong enough feelings for Hasan to go through with this?

Her thoughts were interrupted by one of the servant women who announced that Miss Marjorie Stoughton from the British Embassy was here and wished to see her.

Marjorie Stoughton was tall and fair – unmistakably English. After she had made herself as comfortable as you could on the low stool in the majles, the room used for receiving guests, she stated the purpose of her visit. "Hasan El Sisani came to the Embassy to report your accident and subsequent care here. The Embassy does need to know a few details." Helena nodded.

Marjorie produced a form and a ballpoint pen. After getting Helena's full name and other details in the U.K. Helena suddenly snapped. "Why do you need to know all this?"

Marjorie looked at her – a slow appraising look. "Each year a number of European girls – admittedly a small number, go missing, are attacked, robbed, in this country – it is risky to travel alone – I take it you are travelling alone?"

Helena nodded.

"The Embassy has a great deal of trouble whenever these sort of things happen – investigations, tracking down relatives and so on ......"

"So you think I am at risk in some way?"

"Well, not immediately" said Marjorie "because Hasan Sisani had the good sense to make us aware of your whereabouts."

"Why would he do that?" replied Helena.

"To avoid trouble or misunderstandings – he might have feared you would claim you were being kept against your will."

"What?" said Helena incredulously. There was a long pause in the conversation.

"We have had cases of European girls kept against their will for ransom, for prostitution even." said Marjorie coolly, then more directly "Are you being kept against your will?"

"Not in the slightest" Helena protested. "This family has been very, very kind."

"Good." said Marjorie. She returned to her form and scribbled down some notes. "I would like you to come to the Embassy tomorrow to sign a few forms and meet our security chief – just a formality you know, especially if you plan to continue to travel alone."

After Marjorie had left, Helena mulled over the whole visit – what had it really been about? Was the Embassy that concerned about one backpacker? Possibly; they'd have to follow it up since Hasan had reported her in. Poor Hasan, worried on all accounts that she might prove a complication in his life – a financial burden? – or just trouble with the authorities?

She did not see Hasan that evening – he was away on business to the port of Tangier buying or selling carpets no doubt.

She passed the evening with the women and children. Next day she was guided by Sana, one of the women servants, to the Embassy, as instructed at 10a.m. Leaving Sana to sit in the outer reception she was ushered through the inner reception area until she entered a quiet interior room decorated in English style with armchairs, a sofa, potted plants and heavy drapes – the only Moroccan or Arab element being the richly decorated carpet. Marjorie Stoughton entered by another door. "I've ordered tea, but if you would prefer coffee I can change the order."

Helena hesitated for a moment then said "Tea would be nice."

"Macaulay will join us later." said Marjorie. "He's our security chap."

Marjorie noticed Helena studying the magnificent carpet. "Hasan found it for us." said Marjorie "Isn't it wonderful? – the blue is particularly striking."

Helena had also noticed the intricately worked geometrical flower patterns — she had seen women making these — hours of careful, skillful work.

"Doctor Bin Hassi, Samira, tells me you're out of danger." continued Marjorie after the tea had been brought.

"You know Samira?" enquired Helena.

"We women have to stick together in this country — particularly professional women. Women with total freedom are a rare breed here," said Marjorie, "so yes, I do know her. We often meet at Embassy parties and at hospital staff 'get togethers'."

"I see," said Helena, beginning to realise how foolish she had been to think she was hidden, out of sight, in such a small town as El Kebir.

"Do you know Hasan well?" asked Helena.

Marjorie studied her for a moment as if weighing a reply. "The men here are very handsome, you would even say beautiful — they have good manners and they speak politely — one could be attracted to them," she laughed. "As lovers they are said to be wonderful, but as husbands they can be despots in the home and hypocrites out of it. Islam does not allow the sexes to be free and easy in each others' company out of marriage."

A man entered, and after ushering Marjorie out he introduced himself as Macaulay. "We have run your details through our computer and it appears, Miss Grant, that you are a young woman of some substance, very wealthy in fact." Since Helena did not disagree he went on "Were this fact to be known here you could be in some danger of being kidnapped and held for ransom — some of the interior tribes stick to the old ways."

Helena sighed inwardly. "This is one of the reasons why I am travelling without show or outward sign of wealth," she replied. "Who else knows of this here?"

"Only myself." Macaulay replied.

"Not Miss Stoughton?" she asked.

"No — only I dealt with this file," he said.

"Then I would like you to keep this completely to yourself" she stated.

"Miss Grant, that sort of thing is part of my job," replied Macaulay.

Helena looked at him. "What is the other part of your job, Mr Macaulay?"

"Well," he replied, "to keep an eye on the general situation, on what's going on here."

"So you know the Arab mind?" said Helena.

"The Arab mind, yes, but it's complex." he said.

"A bit like my folk at home — you see I'm from the Western Isles. There are layers of culture, religion, language differences — someone from outside can spend a lifetime getting in — it's like an onion. You think you're there then another layer is revealed — but it's fascinating." "Tell me about Hasan El Sisani." she said.

"The chap you're staying with?" said Macaulay. "Well, he's a successful merchant, carpets. Well known family — not very rich — not very poor. Not an extreme person, not one of your fundamentalists. Marjorie thinks highly of him, but you know the Embassy discourage staff having close personal relationships with the locals when abroad, so it never got off the ground."

Helena found herself strangely relieved. "Do they make good husbands?"

"I think I catch your drift," said Macaulay. He looked at her. "A good man is a good man in any culture — I would rate Hasan a good man."

"What about Islam?" she asked.

"You know, love conquers many barriers." replied Macaulay. "Whatever people say, Islam is not what it once was. It's loosening up — here anyway. We have people in the Western Isles who are probably more strict about their religion than some Muslims. They are great family people here, something we're starting to lose."

Macaulay went on to ask if she planned to stay for a while. He made no comment when she said she probably would stay another month or two. He went over some basic precautions to take if she were to continue travelling alone, then added that he could always be contacted if she was in a jam or needed help of any kind. He gave her his card.

On leaving the Embassy with Sana, Helena adjusted a headscarf to cover her hair and lower face. Even the fact that one person in El Kebir knew about her, strengthened her need to hide away from the wider world – to be hidden, enclosed.

Back at the house she made her way to her room and lay down – the sun was fierce outside but a gentle breeze lazily teased the filmy curtains. Hypnotically they moved to and fro. She dozed and slipped into a dream – she was standing somewhere looking at a large terracotta olive jar – the kind that stood in the corner of the courtyard. They had a voluptuous shape like a single leafed heart, curving gently up, then into the wide mouth. She looked in – it was empty except for a few stray leaves and stones – somehow she felt compelled, and, with a struggle she reached in and took them out – there, it was ready, ready to be filled.

She awoke with a start – the dream was vivid.

That evening she played with the children and talked with Hasan's mother and Yosef's wife Malika. She told them she cared for Hasan – they both smiled and said they knew. She asked about Hasan's plans to marry – no, he had no other woman in his life at this time. They felt he should marry – he was ready for the responsibilities. Hasan's mother said she would welcome Helena as a daughter and Malika would welcome her as a sister. During all their time together in the house the women had bonded in a way that made her feel a warm glow inside.

Dr Bin Hassi called that night. After the usual introductions Helena asked her if she would approach Hasan.

"You have given this serious thought?" said Samira.

"Yes, very serious thought," said Helena. "It is right for me."

"I will see Hasan tomorrow. Goodbye cousin to be." said Dr Bin Hassi smiling as she got up to go.

Two ana a half years later.

Helena stood in the courtyard watching young Ahmed at play. At eighteen months he was toddling across to chase the doves that flew down to drink at the fountain. Inside her she felt the stirring of another new life. She felt secure, with a set of boundaries that both protected, nurtured her and gave her horizons she could touch. Was she content, she asked herself? She was. It was a different life with its own challenges but, she had a family; she had a child, a husband, a home. She felt a fullness. Her wealth lay here – her *real* wealth. She had chosen well.

THE FLOOD

With her right hand she pulled the string back to her cheek. Using the sights she took aim. The bowstring sung as the arrow took flight on its short arc to the target.

She flexed her hand in its encasing leather half glove. The bowstring was so powerful that without the leather it would cut into your fingers.

She had tried to gently exhale that time to reduce the slight shake that holding your breath brings as you fix on the target.

She had strong hands. During the day she worked on a farm carrying pails, bags of feed, shifting bales. Her hands could be gentle too; feeding a calf, stroking a dog, washing an udder.

She was twenty nine, running the bottom of the valley farm single handed since dad had died. It was hard work, long hours – nothing she wasn't used to.

It had been raining for days, dull dreary days, and she'd realised she was getting cabin fever. So when she saw the advert for the archery class on Wednesday night, she turned up.

The hall was brightly lit with huge tulip shaped down lights. "Wouldn't like their electricity bills" she thought, comparing the glare with the weak lights in her own outbuildings.

A mixed bag of locals had stood around while the instructor kitted them all out and gave fairly sparse instructions.

Lined up, arrows began pinging off in all directions, till the instructor told them all to stop. He'd take them all one by one.

While they waited sheepishly for their turn, Chris got chatting to the others. One was Robbie, a neighbouring farmer's son. There were a couple of school kids, then the new district nurse and a chap she'd once nearly run over with a tractor, when his TA unit had been lying down in position in her hayfield. He remembered her with a grin.

Soon they had the basics and were lined up shooting for the rest of the first half of the session so further conversation was minimal. At the break Chris went out into the corridor to the coffee machine. The chap from the TA, was already there getting a hot chocolate. They got talking. She knew him vaguely. He lived up the valley on a small hill farm which he worked with his dad. Sheep mostly. "We've lost a few lambs in the wet" he said, his voice warm and steady. Things had been that bad with prices recently he'd taken a job with the NFU – part time insurance agent. Chris, like many single handed full time farmers didn't have much time for socialising, so she hadn't really had occasion to talk to him before. He was a little taller than her, brown hair, a strong jaw line, hazel eyes and a friendly smile. He stood next to her in the line when they resumed the class. She was conscious of the dark fuzz on his strongly muscled forearm as he drew the bow. The instructor had called him Will, Will Hutton.

By the end of the night her drawstring fingers were sore and her arm ached a little.

Outside it was still teeming down. Everyone dashed for their cars and was off, including Will in his blue Toyota pickup. Chris climbed into the Landrover. Even with wipers on at full it was difficult to see. Spray was being thrown up by small rivers of water running at intervals across the road. Huge puddles had collected on either side. She slowed down.

As she drove off the main road to the farm, she could see in the moonlight the river had come over into the lower meadow field. Nothing strange in that – it happened nearly every year, but it had spread a little further up than usual.

The dogs seemed extra pleased to see her, whining and jumping up. "You want a walk, don't you." she said, realising she'd been away for nearly 4 hours. She wasn't off the farm much and usually the dogs came in the Landrover.

She put on wellies and a coat and went out into the yard, the dogs ahead of her.

In the dimly lit byre the cows seemed peaceful enough, but the pigs were restless, squeaking and snorting. Going through the byre towards the chicken shed out back, she stopped in shock.

The chicken shed was surrounded by a foot of water. The shed lay closest to the riverbank. The river had never come this close — dad would have said something — he had had the farm for 30 years.

As she watched, the chicken shed slowly began to move and drifted silently off into the darkness downstream.

Chris was not the panicking sort but she realised something out of the ordinary was happening.

Back in the house she phoned a neighbour further up the the valley — no reply. She phoned another down the valley. "Yes, its something bad here — we're going to be in real trouble if it don't subside soon" came the reply.

Chris thought for a moment. If the water could rise that far in four hours, then in the next four......? She rang Jake, her neighbour above her on the valley side, to ask if he would help her move stock.

By the time Jake arrived with his son Robbie, she had the cows out on the farm track — Robbie drove them on upwards towards the main road.

The pigs were another story. Battling in the mud with the trailer, they finally managed to get the squealing animals into it.

By now the water was on the byre floor. "I'll just be a minute" said Chris as she dashed back into the house. Behind her she heard Jake drive off briskly up the road with the pigs.

In the kitchen the water was lifting the lino and it squelched as she looked around. What should she try and salvage?

Then a tearing roaring ripping noise like an approaching express train met her ear and next minute water was pouring in the kitchen windows and under the back door.

She rushed to the front door but it wouldn't open — water was spurting under it — through the front windows she could see water half way up them, swirling and dark. The dogs whined. Upstairs quick, she thought and ran two steps at a time to the upper floor, the dogs following.

From the main road Jake and Robbie saw the wall of water, earth, rocks and trees smash into the byre and the house. Jake stood open mouthed but Robbie whipping out his mobile, dialled 112.

He gabbled out what was happening — the operator got him to slow down and give the precise location, "how many were in the house?" she queried.

Chris felt the first real whiff of fear when the lights went out. She huddled with the dogs in her room. Outside the clouds cleared and the moonlight reflecting off the water gave her a spectral view in her wardrobe mirror of the water surging below. All sorts of debris, trees, fence posts, heaving and bobbing on the surface of the water. How high would this water come? The dogs were shaking as she clung to them. The dawn came slow and grey. Through her bedroom door, she saw that the water seemed to have stopped just below the top of the stairs. She stood up — outside she watched as a caravan floated past, then a car, then the carcass of a dead cow. "My god," she thought to herself, "it'll be a miracle if no one is drowned in all of this."

As the light grew stronger she saw, up on the main road, her neighbour's jeep and a blue Toyota, then her cattle in the field just beyond — well that's something. She hung a sheet out of the window to let them know she was still alive.

Then above the sound of the water came the beat of a helicopter's rotors. Something orange was dangling on a taught rope outside the window — a man. She had to use all her strength to open the paint stuck frame. "How many?" he yelled. "One woman and two dogs" she shouted. He disappeared — a basket came down for the dogs. Chris grasped the apparatus in a firm grip and with a lot of difficulty managed to stuff Fluff and Speedy, her collies, into the basket and clip it tight shut.

They vanished aloft. Then the man in orange appeared again. Chris had to wriggle out onto the ledge and cling onto him while he fitted a harness attaching her to his body and then they were off. She looked down –

The farm and steadings were half submerged in a thick grey churning porridge. Debris of all kinds moved on the current. Her Landrover and tractor were nowhere to be seen. Where were the hens by now, she thought with a pang? – probably out at sea.

They took her to an emergency assembly point – her old school as it turned out.

From the stories of the others, the whole valley bottom had been scoured by a wave of rock, mud, and vegetation moving at some speed. The days and days of rain had resulted in a run-off of water – the ground could no longer absorb it, and it had just cascaded straight into the river.

There was devastation up and down the valley – vehicles, mobile homes, sheds and greenhouses, swept out to sea. Premises flooded, filled with mud.

Chris hugged the dogs. Over a cup of tea she shared her experience with people she had known all her life. Robbie appeared with the jeep. "Dad says you can stay with us for now" he said.

Clearing up when the water subsided was heartbreaking. She was insured, but nothing could prepare her for the mud filled hovel that was now her home.

Jake and his son ran her down in their tractor. She stood looking across at the steading and house embedded in a muddy sand bar like a rotting boat. This was going to take ages. Chris's heart sank.

The next day, Jake and Robbie took the front loader and began to scrape the yard and byre free from silt. They found the Landrover upended and wedged against a drystone wall. The tractor had gone. After two days, it was possible to start on the house.

Five of her neighbours came by with barrows and shovels ready to barrow the muck out of the ground floors. It was then that the local insurance agent, Will Hutton, turned up. In front of the neighbours he had said something very profound about the prospects of another flood and the position of the farm. "It might not happen for another 100 years," he had said, "but you wouldn't want your grandchildren to go through what you've just been through, would you?" After he'd gone she got a ribbing, "What's he got on his mind when he's talking about grandchildren Chris?" Chris laughed it off but when they'd all gone, the picture of Will on her farm settled in her mind. He'd never been here before but he seemed to sort of fit, didn't he? What was she doing here on her own anyway? She suddenly felt bleak.

He was quick getting approval for full replacement. She temporarily refurbished the byre and got the stock in. She was able to buy new feed, a tractor and implements and a Landrover. She bought an old caravan to live in for when the builders started on the house. Will seemed to have to visit quite frequently to check on the claim details. She found herself talking a lot with him about the house and the farm – what it meant to her. He was a good listener.

He didn't push her. As a hill farmer his instinct was to be on higher ground.

She wrangled long and hard with herself about the old place. Her past was here, part of her itched to restore it, but she realised what he had said that day in front of the neighbours was right. Also something her father had once said came to her. She had lost a pony years ago and as they buried it he put his arm round her and murmured "there's a trick to life lass, knowing that beginning anew can come out of letting go, as well as from gripping on." She hadn't understood him then.

She finally made her mind up to let go of the old farmhouse and byre and begin again - building near the main road, up the arc of the valley side, with a new house and steading. As for the other, "the gripping on" as Dad had put it, she smiled. Grandchildren were looking to be a distinct possibility now.

Will had finally asked her. Clasping Will Hutton in her arms was an exciting way to begin anew.

LIQUID AND MAGICAL

She stopped the car and got out. The moonlight glinted on the metalled road. Around her the still night of the glen in summer, the low dark hills clearly visible. She took a deep breath. The air was fresh, soft, the smell of damp heather and bracken sharpened with a tang of willow.

As the sound and vibration of the engine ebbed away from her body, she found the silence receded as the night sounds crept in. A tawny owl woo wooed, then off to her right the mournful crushed cry of a fox in the pinewoods.

What was that? In the background steadily murmuring – of course, a river, down to the left in the valley bottom. She imagined it dark and rippling over smooth boulders. The sound and taste of hill water were things she missed most in the city.

She shivered a little in her duffle coat. As she turned to open the car door she froze as she saw on the silvery ribbon of the road three dark shapes close and for a moment menacing like grown men with their hands held up. Then they shifted position and she saw the sheen of the moon on their flanks and the antlers, branch like, against the sky. Red deer stags, cautious, stopping to check her out as they crossed the road. One of them coughed. Their hooves clicking delicate steps they moved off slowly, a faint swishing of the undergrowth marking their progress.

What was it like to be them at night, stepping dainty on hooves through this landscape, nostrils keenly alert, ears vibrating to the slightest nuance of sound?

She stood by the car, the door unopened. Why was it nature could do this, reach into your very soul and fill you with awe and wonder. It was almost too much to take, like a grief memory deeply buried bubbling to the surface overwhelming you with feeling.

Did we live a day-to-day life in a desensitised zone? Had there been an earlier life when people walked like the deer in the landscape, feeling it, hearing it, smelling it so intensely they were one with it. Yes, that was it, she thought, the feeling of oneness – our modern sense of individuality is so strong we avoid, resist, deny that oneness, that merging with the greater whole, glimpsing it only fleetingly when we are alone, when we are gripped by intense feeling, in love, grief or joy, or when we are very small and the boundaries between ourselves and the world are still liquid and magical.